IBSN 9780646873688

FOUR TOLD.

By R.M.Davis.

Contents-

(1)

I'll NEVER LEAVE YOU.

Dirty small hooves on pink bristled legs tapped aimlessly in the foliage on the damp ground. Wet leaves fallen and blown into small gatherings at bases of saplings and dead tree trunks, long since fallen. No longer upright. Bent, rotting, reminiscent of lean-to's. Vines ambled, twined and latching. Roping the branch's remains, grasping and imprisoning them. Creating labyrinths of clutter and open spaces, new growth forming hiding spaces, compost covering mud. Beetles, ants, skinny legged native spiders, the hair-width legs on primal alert. The minutest creatures unencumbered by comparatively gigantic mammal offspring rooting about the forest bush bed.

 Discarded webs among leaves or wild-grasses, too wispy to be seen, unfelt by spiky skinned coats of the piglets, mooning about in their absent minded snuffling, snorting breathes inward, mindless of other small noises about them. Insensitive to the usual cracks of wood and shuffles of the parent boars. Three or four young piglets sniffed and rooted happily, unable to anticipate the oncoming danger. Fifty metres away the mother falls into a trap. Jolts wildly, crashes against restraints. Rear leg slashed ruthlessly, held fast by metal claws hammered fast to a tree root.

Squealing is too slight a verb, screams piercing, tendons pulled into ribbons. Padlocked fast in iron vice between bones, ankle anchored, body thrown upright. Anger succeeding terror, rage. Obliterating humiliation and fright. This sudden violent onslaught of action, vicious, instantaneous, the terrifying noise, the scent of instincts sent the nearby offspring dashing, unawares of direction. Unable to discern if they were still in a group, running, fleeing, the signal they heard trumpeted from the mother, one of survival, with one directive, escape. Scattered, dispersed into bushland, intelligible distance covered. Panting the wild pig siblings abandoned.

On following hours and days surviving hogs will regroup together again in the bush terrain, the mother knew it. She fought beyond brevity, beyond any sense, adrenaline rising and subsiding the right of the wound, aborting feeling, prepared for the battle, of refusing any surrender. If her captors wanted her, she would fight. Grunts and screams continued until all energy was lost, the primeval instincts blotting out what animalistic understanding there is of full thoughts, the outer wails overwhelming the other parental screaming. The inner animal spirit sounding under the sirens of it all, "I'll never leave you".

The sadistic smirk and sneer of the men lingered, listening to the ebbing fight of sinew and metal. They knew that blood loss was not what they patiently waited for. It was shock, a state of protective exhaustion that will eventually overcome the hog. Or boar. Only a closer personal inspection of the slay would define that. A boar might be dangerous, gnashing wildly, might reef itself from the traps teeth, may fight back longer, sever arm or hand from man's body with its own bared teeth. Make no difference when it came to gutting or eating though. A pig is a pig is a pig.

 Sounds quieted down, settled in the trees around them. One of the white men pulled a ring tab from the top of a beer can. Objectives achieved they were free to move about a little, release some foreign scents into the natural air. Move their booted feet across sticks and debris. The other was the older brother, he was the one who would give the all clear, the nod, that he was satisfied with his perverse interlude. He was not afraid of being torn by furious tusks. He just savoured and enjoyed the ability to kill things. The younger brother sighed and sat back on the vertical log, waiting for the go ahead. His thought strayed to the woman waiting for them back in the car. It wasn't his woman, but being near to her, bathed in her company was more desirable to him than waiting out his brothers tranced reverie. An hour passed, they stayed like that. One sitting, drinking, dreaming, the other standing straight up where he was, caught in some state of undecipherable pause. Then the earth came back to him, and actions commenced again. Nate stepped forward without warning, the other smiled and threw down his empty drink can into the bushes. Followed him towards the now silent direction of the thrashed beast. They had the kill, together they dragged it back to the clearing and cut and tied it, then quietly walked back to where they had parked the vehicle.

A young woman with blonde hair seated inside got out of the front seat where she had been patiently waiting, reading her book. She smiled at the two men, both of them equally. Deftly moved to place herself into the back seat, without need for instruction, she didn't mind the peaceful atmosphere of the bush, but was also now glad the boys had completed the game, as daylight was fading and she still had some chores to attend to back at home. And a bottle of wine waiting for her chilled in her refrigerator. No drinking was allowed for her by Nate until the hunts were completed, she was expected to stay in full control of her facilities in case there was some emergency requiring her to take over the driving. This never happened but it could, and she had no preference for the few cans of ale her brother-in-law had left warming on the floor of the car.

Nate had that self-satisfied calmness he attained after each successful primal mission. She had learned a while back that these afternoons ran a lot smoother if she neglected to complain about the warm smell of dead animal, the longer she could keep the silence on the trip back home, the more likely Nate would stay in this lulled manner. To whinge or criticise him for any blood-mess's left to pool and stain the rear carrier of the vehicle, (warmed by friction of wheel rotation and motor operation, sending metallic smells into her awareness) was a folly as the next mood hedging in on the peripheral could be excitable, if not managed well and brought about too suddenly.

The car pulled into the driveway of the front yard. Hovered beside the front path, allowed Katie to climb out of the rear passenger side door. The back door swung open and she stepped around it. Percy passed out the Esky to her and slid across the backseat pulling a backpack and a half case of beer back out with him. Percy followed Katie along the front path and clamoured through wooden framed screen door, left unlocked. There was a front door that stood open, in a small town like theirs every person knew who lived in each house, who owned it, who rented from who. Their rented weatherboard two bedder was a bank lease, the primary school that employed Nate, Katie and Percy always leased the same address to whoever was the standing Principal, or to teachers who had been in town for less than five years. They qualified in both regards.

The car backed up back out of the driveway in reverse, crept onto the street, and over the curb, moved through the empty lot next door and coming to a standstill by the rear fence line. The empty lot had no rear fence, edged onto the sports oval attached to the behind of the primary school. There was a small narrow ditch between oval and Nate's back fence line so this was as close to the back yard's gate as the car could park, not that it mattered as no one used the lot for anything and there was no resident in the house on the other side of it.

Percy and Katie had moved through the hallway passage, Percy held open the fridge, Katie took cans from the carton Percy had in his other hand. Two by two Katie stacked beers into the fridge door, she bent down lower and reached into the middle shelf and tugged out a plastic bag of vegetables she was going to cut up for their dinner. She straightened up as Percy tossed the empty carton onto the floor beside the fridge. They heard Nate cut the engine in the car. He had come to a stop. Percy lifted his now free hand and pushed back a loose lock of Katie's hair that had slipped free of her loose bun. She looked straight ahead into Percy's eyes. No words were needed. No expressions changed. There was no need for words. Percy moved his other hand from the fridge's door and Katie stepped out of the opening. She stepped around him and put the vegetable bag on the bench. Katie picked up the chopping board from the sideboard and reached into a drawer for a sharp knife. Her hand shook. Percy closed the refrigerator door and looked down at the floor,

"Don't worry, I'll stay here tonight, okay? I'll never leave you". She nodded, he continued through the hall, pushed the back screen, out the door into the yard.

 The grass grew in patches. The dry had created dust patches from the lack of care. No one cared about the little dirt space, no one was ever at home during the daytimes, no children had played in this yard for years. Percy crossed the yard and vaulted over the fence, landing next to Nate who already had his hands on one end of the hog's body, waiting. Percy gripped the other two hoofs covered by a canvas tarp and together hauled the dead body free from the boot, over the fence, dropping it evenly in same moment, to land inside the back yard. Inside Katie heated water in a pot, began slicing potatoes, dropping the vegie into salted water. Minutes later she appeared on the back veranda, and started lighting citronella candles on the tables, positioning a row of them like chess pieces, between the grass line and the kitchen window and back door. She knew the blood, stickiness and smell of dead entrails was going to bring a swarm of flies into the area, and was preparing her defences in advance. Percy didn't watch her, keeping up with Nate for this next part. He did not look at Katie. Katie did not linger to watch Percy helping Nate.

The pot steamed through the lid as Katie held it fast to the saucepan with a tea towel in her other hand. Drained the potatoes, peas, scooped them out onto the serving plates. Withdrew the baking tray from the oven, careful of spitting fats she forked the roasted meats onto the wooden bread board, carved out some hunks, placed the good meats beside the peas. Flour into fat, water into flour, stirred up some home-made gravy with her wooden spoon, ladled the rich mixture generously across three plates. Lifting the remaining baked pork back into the tray to swim in thickened flavour, gravy, luxuriant, back into the oven until later.

 Balancing Percy and Nate's plates together Katie walked their meals out the back door and placed them beside each man, on the wooden dining table on the back veranda.

"Thanks love," Percy didn't look at her but started exhuming his platter immediately. Nate gave no recognition or acknowledgment of her, still staring into the back yard. Nate watched blood dripping with a slowing regularity, from the upended hog, now slashed out and hanging from a large metal butchers S-hook, slung into the hooves at one end, suspended from a chain link at the other end, the chain looped over a branch coming straight out of an old sturdy gum tree at the end of the yard. The sticky carcass spewed shredded flesh tubes from below its ribcage where Nate had butchered through twin rows of teat's and severed guts, exposing stomach, offal's and bladder system.

A myriad of twined bloated sausages of intestines, veiny sacks and globule's. disgusting fragrances of bile and shit, pooled into a floating pile on the dirt and grass below it. Katie ducked inside again, and returned to them with her own plate. She placed the plate on the table opposite where Nate was situated, and moved about the veranda repositioning the line of candles to better ward off the fly defensive from the dinner table.

Under the table Percy shifted his boot against Nate's foot. The disturbance shouldered Nate out of his personal reverie, snapped him from some trance like state back into present reality. He shook his head clear, turned his chair square to the table, picked up his knife and fork and started his dinner. Percy took his cue from his brother and between fork-full he opened up a conversation with Katie drawing Nate into it with a few well engineered and structured queries. Relief and relaxation stole over her, who enjoyed the moment, lived for the moments like this. Nate paused halfway through his dinner, rose from the table and left them just long enough to switch on the stereo to the music station on the radio, sat back down to finish his plate and intermittently participating in the conversation going on between Percy and Katie. These were the easy parts, when they all felt at ease and not in competition with each other. No, that wasn't the right description; was the steering wheel envious of the axle of the wheels? They were parts of the same functioning unit. Unable to move forward without the mechanism of the other, each providing a vital and valued function and element, mute and dysfunctional without the accompaniment of the other two, however separate and distinctive they were from each other. They were made to be assembled together, unable to move forward without the other parts of itself.

There had been attempts and trials of separation's, between the brothers, of the marriage, resistance's to the mental and emotional bonds that combined the three of them, into a unit that only they could understand and together an acceptance that no other societal set up would give them their approval. They became forged and determined to reject the seeking of approval from any others. Became a trio of loners, able to exist right in the glaring eye of society, gaining employment in highly visible social positions, school teacher, principal, janitor and groundsman, social worker for the governing department, preferring state schools. Hiding their vulgarities in plain sight by taking prominent public positions in small rural communities, where things move slowly, actions against them even slower.

Resuming his place at the table in front of his plate, Nate complimented Katie on her meal. Percy went and fished some cans of ale from the fridge in the kitchen dumping his empty plate into the sink. Came back out and hooked himself into a swinging rope hammock tied onto the back balcony rails, the other end tethered to a fence post. Katie smiled and took both hers and Nate's now empty plate's to the kitchen. Came back out via the laundry room. In her hands she held two little puppies, Katie stepped quietly down the rear step, off veranda onto dirt, padded over patchy grass clumps and down the back yard. She bent down and placed the two small dogs on the ground near the pool of blood. Nate watched, approved, nodded to himself. Gladdened by the effort, this action of Katie was met with approval, but he wouldn't say it. Nate was pleased that he didn't have to prompt her. She was performing.

He called out to her, "I'm going out, don't wait up". Nate turned to Percy, "You staying, yeah?". Percy nods. "Take care of her, don't let her leave". Percy nods, turns his gaze towards Katie, who was returning from where she had set down the little pups. She looked at Nate, "I'll never leave you."

Nate didn't reply. Turned on his heel and travelled down the hall and out of the front door. Percy reached his hand out from the hammock, grasped Katie's fingers and tugged, she allowed herself to be pulled, climbing into the hammocks wide net, half to the side of, half on top of Percy's chest. She nested her face into his shoulder and pushed his foot against the fence palings, sending them both into a slow rocking sway and swing. The pups lapped around in the blood-mud. The fly's buzzing clear of the citronella in the air.

Nate walked down the hallway and departed via the front door. Leaving his car parked at the rear of the house, no need to lock it up in this poorly populated rural town. He secretly wished someone would try and take it, give him a reason and outlet for his anger. He ambled down his path and turned right at the gate, taking the long way around, along his street, turning right again when he reached the corner of the sidewalk. Barely even a foot path here, just a treading down of grass that led around the block to the other end of the road, ending in the gravel carpark area in front of the state school where he worked. As Principal no one would question him as to why someone had entered the grounds so late in the evening, it was his usual habit. Nate busied himself emptying some garbage bins from the front quadrangle as he went along, dumping contents into the industrial sized dumpster at the edge of the buildings. Slowly walked back placing the few now empty receptacles back into their positions. Dusted his hands, already dirty with blood stained nail beds, on the front of his jeans. Put his hands on his hips and leisurely slow he perused his environment.

Feeling in control, no one for him to answer to in this place. Satisfied with himself, turning towards the building he let himself in with his own keys. Nate took up his spot at his wooden desk and began shuffling papers, reading some notes, moved on to correcting papers of the students. The first pile he worked through briskly, absent-mindedly, the second manila folder on the desk was not belonging to a class of his. He examined the work of Katie's classes students. Frowning and creasing his brow he corrected and altered her markings for her, though her assessments were not incorrect. Nor was Katie lazy or running behind in her own assigned work. This was just for his purpose, with these pen markings he made sent their own message, not to the students but particularly to let her know, in all regard, that every movement, action, pen-stroke was seen. That he had the final say about everything in her life. Her day. Nate monitored and oversaw each thought she had, any decision, his power was all, her boundaries of his creation. This theme he enforced by containing her, controlling everything, even her assessment of her students, her teaching, her movements, her lunch break, her sleeping, her breathing, Nate had to let her know that he was the master of it all. And that was why he was tending to small duties at this moment, so that tomorrow during the school day there would be little for him to have to do, and he could stay stationed outside her classroom while she taught. She belonged where he told her to be. He prepped the lesson for tomorrow, and went to her classroom and placed the notes on her desk.

Throughout the night he also completed several of Percy's janitorial duties, lest he be distracted by his own employment during the day and therefore not at Nate's immediate disposal, Percy would step up and keep watch over Katie in the case of Nate having to give his direct attention to some student or matter that would distract him from being ever present at his wife's locations. He did not see this as excessive, just liked to be in control. Nate thought of his wife for a moment, "Kate, I'll never leave you" he whispered under his breath.

Percy edged himself from underneath Katie, rolling her onto her back in the hammock, she curled into herself and allowed the netting to hug her small frame as Percy extracted himself and became upright. He bent and pulled on his boots, stomped down the grass and scooped up the sleeping puppies from the messy grass. Took them into the laundry to give them a shallow warm bath, easing crusted blood drops from the jaw, paws and belly's. Towelled them dry and dropped them lovingly into the cardboard box lined with old towels that was on the cement floor of the laundry next to the washing machine. He took down the hunting knife and the boner from the windowsill and went back to the hog's carcass to finish the job. It was coming daylight when the meat was cut.

Katie roused herself from the hammock and without instruction went to the kitchen drawers, got out the plastic bags, wiped down the dining table and covered it with a few large green garbage bags. Percy transferred the cuts of pork to the table and Katie began placing sections into bags, sealing them and depositing the haul into a deep chest freezer in the kitchen, which sat they supposed, where the dining table should have lived.

From the far side of the football oval Nate sat on the ground, watching them work quickly, quietly, harmoniously together. Waited until the task was over and Nate observed the two leave the back balcony moving out of his view into the house, he saw the light come on through the bathroom window pane, obscured by the fly screen and the inner curtains. Nate held back, allowed them their space.

Half an hour passed by, Nate rose up and crossed the sports oval travelling from school grounds side to his house, tapping on the roof of his car as he crossed the fence line and inside. He stepped towards the bathroom door, removed his clothes and let them fall to the hall way floor. Percy stood facing him, his arms wrapped around Katie, her head resting again on Percy's shoulder letting the water fall over her head down her face, eyelids closed, the steam enveloping them in rising caresses, Percy pushed open the glass door of the shower stall, turned himself and Katie in small movements, not disturbing her but shifting the direction of their access so that now her forehead was visible to Nate. And he stepped forward and Percy shifted her weight from his chest and eased himself back, out of the steamy stall one foot at a time as Nate sidled inwards and took over Percy's position. Nate's arms slid around Katie's torso and she raised her arms to hang herself from around his neck. Percy reached to a towel hanging from the door, dried himself off and tucked the towel around his waist, stepped out of the steamed up room into the cooler air of the hallway.

Percy poked about in the kitchen, assembled some breakfast and coffee, passed by the couple's bedroom to snag a fresh shirt and a pair of jeans. He was sitting on the lounge in front of the T.V. when Katie and Nate emerged from the bathroom and went about their morning rituals. Without conversing Nate fixed his own coffee and followed his footpath trail back to the school in time to unlock the buildings entrances and usher in the teachers for them to begin the mornings tutorials, and stood in front of his office doors impatiently, on the pretext of greeting students being led in by their parents into another day's education. From his vantage point he witnessed Percy delivering Katie from the rear oval into a side building where her classroom was situated. At the outer of the building Percy left her to go about his own business, something to do with petrol and a ride on lawn mower, the ongoing maintenance of the oval's lawns. Children milled about in the hall ways, waiting for the bell signifying morning assembly.

With Nate stationed at the front of the school, and Percy at the rear of the grounds, Katie sat at her desk in her classroom, numb in a meditative silence, lifting the corners of her mouth briefly at each small child that filed into the room, not rushing them, happy to let them muck about, be themselves, gave them licence to spend a few minutes without being directed and orchestrated by instruction.

"Leave them be", the words echoing through her mind, her empathy completely sympathetic in relation to her own personal feelings at that moment. The constraints of her own parameters a suffocating constricting weight getting heavier each day. She wondered what would happen when this compressing sphere shrunk its diameter to its centre nucleus. "Do I implode?" she wondered, "Like a black hole in space, do I turn inside out, do I shatter, inwards, or explode?" Katie visualised the vortex of emotion at her centre. Seen it as a physical thing, the shattering shards of atoms imagined as millions of tiny bits of reflecting glass, dissipating her into the atmosphere, no gravity around it.

"Miss?". A child's voice breaks into her reverie, Katie snaps back into the present, swallows the lump in her throat. Smiles. Proceeds with her day. Outside her window the hum and drone of a lawn mower, the sound moving closer and then receding in a regular pattern. She knew it was Percy, also knew that outside her classroom door Nate would be within line of sight. She didn't question this, already knew the answer and pulled mentally into herself, imagined a cardboard carton being placed over her head, a virtual container, it's limits confining her. She hadn't realised the thought fully yet had not recognised it as a full idea, but silently the concept had started budding, unconsciously the countdown had commenced. This was her inner clock going into a countdown, to a point I time when she would no longer be in suspension, suspended animation as it were. This is the internal survival instinct, allowing one self to endure the present suffocation, dulling all sense of repressive torture's. A body lying in wait.

Katie switched off her white noise and promptly found herself back in her classroom. She hit the reset button, put her focus on the little faces in front of her, gave the children the time and attention they deserved. Used the youthful enthusiasm to bolster her reserve, pad out her spirit and occupy her mind, pushing away from herself the knowledge that Nate was 100% certainly standing in the corridor outside her classroom, shoved him far, far away until 3 o'clock when she had to say goodbye to her little one's for the afternoon. Her stomach rumbled, she had stayed inside the room during recess and lunchbreak. Nate wanted her to stay inside a box, she would stay in the fucking box. More and more she found herself surprised by these little thoughts, retaliating inwardly even though her conscious decision was still to go along with what was happening to her.

Outside the Principal's office Percy called to Nate through his office door, "You in there?",

"Nope" replied Nate not from the office but from the corridor behind Percy, coming from the direction of Katie's classroom. Nate reached Percy and opened up the door marked Principal, they both stepped inside. Percy looked to Nate. Nate looked down to the carpeted floor.

"Right", Percy took his cue, "I'll get her, go home". Nate nodded his head, left the room. Percy shoved his hands into the pockets of his jeans, waited a beat or two, sighed and headed back through the Principal's door, down the halls and opened up the door to Katie's first graders class, she still sat at her desk, back straight, unmoving, pen in hand above a sheet of paper. This pose intended to give any onlooker the image that she was involved in some task, perched at her desk. But anyone who watched for a minute, was in any way observant, would see something else, her motionless reverie would indicate something else, a screaming urgency, begging for help, an unanswered siren.

Percy came over to her desk, took her by her arm gently, "Come on babe", he smoothed her into standing, led her out the door and down the hall onto the path, back into her house, "Stop it" said Percy. He turned to face her when they had entered the lounge room. "Katie!", Percy shouted. The noise woke her from her trance like state like a slap to the face. Her eyes focused on Percy's eyes and then she smiled. A real smile, "That's it, babe", Percy laughed outward, hugged her and shook his head. It was like she was getting further away each time, it frightened him. He knew that he could not keep avoiding taking some action, the present situation wasn't working, Nat was the only one who seems to be appeased.

"Let's have a beer, it's been too hot today". They turned all the blinds down, air conditioner up, he collected beers and wine from the fridge and made a little haven of sorts by shutting themselves away into the lounge room. Television on, a little normality, later Nate would join them, but not before Percy had helped her shake off the mood of the day.

A few hours later in the evening, Percy lifted Katie's sleeping body from the arm chair. Left Nate to sleep on the lounge. Carried her to the bedroom and placed her gently on her bed. He crept back out of the room quietly and let himself out of the front door, leaving them to their sleep. Small whine's leaked through the laundry door and into the hallway but went unheard. The three of them had neglected the puppies that day. Hungry sounds tapered off, picking up again in the early hours before sunrise.

Her eyes startled open, Katie looked up into a livid Nate's face. A heavy hand of steel held her head down flat to the pillow, she felt surely as though he would crack the top of her skull with the weight. Using the full leverage of his body held above hers, forcing her immobile, Nate had one hand over her forehead and the other cupped over her closed mouth, holding her jaw shut, she felt a crack in her neck. Became terrified. Her brain screamed wildly, 'He's going to snap my fucking neck'. Nate continued his pushing down into her while he yelled and spat profanity in front of her face. She couldn't quite make it out, the words like thunder strung together and anxiety and flooding panic prevented her from deciphering the glaring sounds. He thought she had done something. But what it was did not matter, when he became like this her fool protests and reasons were futile, useless. Katie felt the blackness closing over her eyes slowly before the dizziness fully took hold of her brain. White glitter filtered through a smoked haze, at the verge of unconsciousness. She felt all of the weight lift off of her in a sudden unexpected motion.

Percy had heard Nate going ballistic as he came into the front yard. His own brand of fear shot through him, sensing Katie's danger and responding instantly. He flew up the steps and propelled through the front door, not bothering with the handle, cracked the soft wood of the door jam in a fluid response, adrenaline seized him.

Nate didn't see it coming, was too absorbed in his frantic menace. Thinking he was alone with her, and had jumped at the opportunity. Percy cleared the bed, pushed out his booted foot so that it connected first with Nate's chin. Lifted him clear off of her. Percy didn't hesitate, gained his footing and lurched his torso over Nate's still in motion body. The men grappled and fought an aggression, mindless of obstacles and furnishings knocked and damaged in the progress. Struggle continued for minutes, both of them found themselves not standing, but on their knees. Striking blows to the others face, blood streaked a split lip, bruises flourished. Percy had gripped onto Nate's arms. His damage was the worst due to the initial well placed kick to the jaw. Nate paused and drew in a deep haggard breath. Percy used this gap to centre him. They looked at each other and in a split second Nate perceived that Percy seemed to be looking at him, but the slightest fraction of movement in the eye and he comprehended that even though Percy was turned towards him he was actually seeming to look through him. Past him, at something positioned just behind Nate's head, not in his view. Percy didn't falter, kept his position and said very quietly and surely, "I'll never leave you".

In that same instant Nate registered that Percy wasn't talking to him, the walls of the bedroom seemed to expand and then contract, like a scene from a movie with a time-tunnel. Katie pushed the barrel of the pistol against the nape of Nate's neck. Gunpowder cracked. "I know" she said.

CHARITY.

Shaking the irritation built up in the interior of her brows, blinked her eyes behind spectacles. A mental push of brain, mind over matter, blocking the impatient stem of negative, tiresome thought clogging the conscious inch between the forehead and the temple area above her ears. "Goddamned paperwork". Unable to help from glancing sideways to the left of the desk. A table clock shows 2. Two more hours, knowing that the strong desire to keep checking the time piece just adds to the agony. A watched pot never boils. Gail's paid position at her not-for-profit organisation was taken in the pretence of inner satisfaction, a false lure surely providing a change from her former position as a bank clerk. Fantasy. Ruse. Governing councils, data entry, policy, procedure, steel desk, numbers and endless requests. "Swapped the name on the pay sheet, did stuff-all", she swears to herself. Over it. Weary. Impervious to it all. Housing officer, sounds official. The title suggesting that the community minded role is going to help people, house people. People in need. The cynicism passed down from Gail's father has seeped into her way of thinking, "Become a pen pusher for the dole bludgers". Daddy wasn't far wrong it seems. Requests, unpaid accounts, evictions, ungratefulness, vandalism of properties. This is what she sees now. Not faces, just names, account number this, reference number that, invoices, items, repair orders, more data entry, rat, rat, rats. Six days before Christmas, her own personal holiday less than two hours away.

Tap tap. "Gail, can you come down to the lunch room, I want you to meet somebody". Wendy stands in her office doorway, quietly waits for Gail to push her chair back, stand and follow her out to the corridor. Gail wants to ask what's going on but, this, is over rid by the boon of a few minute's distraction from her desk. Wendy guides her past the staff lunch room, further on, passing into the volunteer's tea room. Gail looks to Wendy, raised her eyebrows in silent query. Wendy barely nods, leads them to a seat at the factory made Formica table. A pierced and tattooed man in denim shorts half turns from the sink, finished with the kettle. Wendy pretends to be immersed in her selection of a biscuit from the plate in the centre of the table. Gail watches this with a low level of interest. "Blimey, churchie's and their need for socialising", she thinks, raises her wrist to gauge her watch.

"Still here Mike?" Wendy proffers. A nod. Scruffy hair, smudged cheek, faded black Iron Maiden t-shirt. He hesitates to move forward. Does not take a seat at the table, stands awkwardly, eyes averted. "I thought a saw you this morning", she continues, addressing him again, "were you walking past that servo in Grays Wood?", a nod, he shrugs. Wendy continues "I was dropping my husband to work, he's in that Industrial section". Nothing. Mike dunks a biscuit in his tea, still on his feet. Eyes averted. "Would have been pretty early, before 6". Gail pulls a cream cookie from the plate. Remembers herself, grasps in the air. "How many days a week do you work here Mike?", she manages. He turns back toward the stainless steel sink, rinses his cup, Wendy jumps in for him. "Mike's here five days, warehouse opens at seven". Gail looks to Wendy, "7 until 5. That's 10 hours. Five days a week". The rest of her calculations are done in her head. Grays Wood is 16 km away. This guy walks from there, into town, daylight starts, late finishes. Seems to be embarrassed by helping himself to a biscuit. Wendy waits for the penny to drop. Grays Wood is not a residential area. There are no homes in that section, it doesn't make sense.

Then it hits. Gail shook her head, the smile slowly stretches across her face. She gets it now. Wendy is still faking it with her biscuit.

"Mike, I'm Gail, I'm going to need you to come with me, back to my office".

(3)

BALD CORINNE.

Unassuming. Short, ordinary, one of the people whom would make up part of a crowd but you never actually see her. Forgotten in the moment your eye's moved over her. Never pausing your sight to fall on her. Passed over without actual thought. There was nothing visually exceptional about her. Her art was one of blending in. The truest intention of her heart was never to be a bother to anyone. She succeeded. Never quarrelled, never gave unsolicited advice, quiet temperament. Was not disrespectful, argumentative. A shrug of the shoulders and quick supportive agreement. Not intentionally funny, a giver. A miser, once a wife, a mother to two or three I believe. Although the children had grown taller than her by the time I met her, everyone had.

2014. I came to live in a small country town of Queensland, inland of the Sunshine Coast. An unplanned geographical from interstate, fate and addiction forced me to relocate, begin again as it were. Newborn in tow, determined not to recreate mistakes of the past, alone and bereft of all my possessions, I brought with me one suitcase containing only the essentials belonging to my baby. Anyway, this is not about me. So, I landed, willing to accept any form of accommodation, my budget low and only having the stipulations that I was the only tenant. Able to shut the door, be safe and house my baby.

Two options were available in this town, for people with my income. The grimy rooms above a local hotel in the main street, a sure fire place to rouse authorities interest in me, who would then surely remove my baby from me and such an unsuitable venue, or, a dodgy caravan park that sat ten kilometres outside of the town. The lowest form of society lived there, on the outskirts, in between a cemetery and a service station on a road that was previously a section of the old highway. To be fair it wasn't just lowlifes, there were others like me, thrown out from their lives, using this dump as the pit stop to a better world. But the majority were people given up on life, alcohol addictions managed in shoddy comfort, seniors fighting the system, clinging to last year's refusing old aged homes and the like. Unfortunate people.

No nightly rentals, it was week to week, permanent rates that equalled our pensions and levelled our intentions. Two metre by three metre wooden cabins, without kitchens or bathrooms dotted along the dirty track serving for a road around the park. No kiosk, no running water inside, we were adequately grateful to be supplied with a clothes line, a toilet block and a telephone box in front of the service station. My cabin was positioned next to both the line and the lavatory block, first cabin on the left upon entry to the park. This afforded me to have a view of everyone entering and exiting through the boom gate. All traffic passed by my door. This would deter me from having my door open, leaving the little room and myself visible for inspection. As my baby grew to toddler I could no longer keep him inside the 2m square space that housed my single bed, cot and bar fridge. I recall with astonishment that we even fit in there.

So days progressed to sitting at a little metal table on my cabins veranda, book in hand, telling my boy play on the grass under the clothes line. This is where I sat when Corinne approached me the first time. Cornered as I was, the little lady turned her attentions to my son, smiling and talking to him to get his attention. I did pretend to be awfully busy and absorbed in my book. This place was a place one kept to themselves. Destitute neighbours always wanting to borrow something, inviting me for a 'drink', or fighting amongst themselves quite openly in the street, the ploughed dusty road.

Corinne never asked me for anything, and was irritatingly cheerful enough that she couldn't be ignored. Soon she became a regular passer-by. Always with a smile, a greeting and some praise for my little boy. Eventually out of the chit chat I learnt that she had children too, grown now. Not much information about the elder but always expressed concerns for her daughter, caught up in bad relationships, drug issue's, possible pregnancies, etc. I kept my responses short and sweet, not really wanting to involve myself, or show too much interest for fear of encouraging further talking. I only had one goal, to keep my head down and my life uncomplicated. As my life would have it, my plans of isolation were futile, because life moves around us like pesky winged bugs, dashing like moths, zeroing in on us despite our uselessly swatting the buzzing insects away. Their goal is too sting us, disrupt and reposition us. Bleed us or remove us.

My little child was understandably becoming restless, day by day he became more intrigued and curious, as toddler's minds do. It became harder and more energy consuming to keep him amused in our little space, tiny hands find all and tiny feet seek more ground. The books became less read, and my imagination and tolerance more drawn upon. One morning like this we drew battle lines in the shade, he more determined than I to win. Common sense of an onlooker shaking their head, could enlighten any mother that it was futile, to keep a child restrained. Nothing was going to stop him from reaching the dirt road in front of the veranda. Those small slate rocks and twigs too fascinating to resist tough. So his strategy simple, if he threw his toys over the balcony rail, into the dirt below then he could be forgiven for retrieving them, thus one step closer to the goal destination, railing, dirt, road, farewell... Dutiful mommy giving allowance several times, rising to standing, down the 2-steps, admonishments given, being part of his game, his amusement.

Fish the toy from the dust, chiding, gullible interaction, retreat up 2-step, return the toy, sit, lift my book, repeat, repeat.

In one of these rotations I was standing two feet in the dust, bent over tin truck, when he pushed his head through balcony railings to swat at me. Two chubby sets of fingers grasped wooden pole either side of his head. Cheeky grin, giggles, soon turned to confusion, panic, fear. His round head stuck, I tested the strength of the railings, my anxiety level sky rocketing while trying to keep outward calm and not encourage further agitation in him. I frantically looked about, it was early morning. No one in sight. The dusty thoroughfare was deserted. I contemplated running the forty odd metres up to the boom gate and office but I didn't want to leave him unattended. I wasn't even sure if anyone was in the office yet, and to do this was guaranteed to incite instant panic in him. I was using all my mental clarity to disguise my own distress.

The dilemma must have been heard or perhaps it was just luck, coincidence or good fortune, suddenly Corinne appeared at my side. I hurriedly explained, though it was clear to see, running through some options of some emergency. I needed not to, Corinne was in front of his face, she bent over, placing her face below his and attention diverted, he smiled and his eyes followed her curly hair. Stealthily Corinne's hand came up quickly to the side and gently bopped him on the forehead. Not seeing her hand coming he pulled backwards and upwards to rear from the felt but unseen tap on the head. Little blonde ringlets and rosy cheeks smoothed straight out of the restraining bars, (despite my having tried all possible conceivable angles for removal). Just like that Corinne extinguished my horrific scenes of ambulance men with cutting saws which were envisioned in my head, flashing anticipated drama's I hope not unlike other parents may experience. Alarm now abated, relief and gratitude flood me. Strange that the face of a person whom I scarcely knew becomes the saviour of the moment. My inner dread had prevented me from calmly coming to a solution, however a quick trick of distraction eased us from tragedy to saved. Any mother can tell you the adrenaline that overcomes the senses when offspring are threatened, followed by the release of tensions immediate upon removal of perceived dangers.

This event provided the gateway for me, to change my first impressions of the four foot something woman from nuisance to useful. It could never be labelled a 'grand gesture'. It was just a few moments of an ordinary day, unplanned, unexpected, undrafted. Inconsequential to everyone but me. At his young age this would not be a memory imprinted for my boy, no other neighbours witnessed and when I recalled the day years later, even Corinne responded "Did I? I don't remember that". What Corinne did remember was his cherub face, pretty curls, his smile and me. That's how she was. Never the type to extract praise, always shrugged off compliments. Decreeing deeds as 'nothings', "That's what we are supposed to do, aren't we?". A quick blink and any thankyou was dispersed up into the air as if the attention received was a weight on her to be resisted.

The usual routine's continued. What changed was my openness and my attitude. Now I gave Corinne my attention when she happened passed. On a different occasion during this new friendship she arrived at the veranda, carrying a set of heavy backed curtains. I don't know where they came from, maybe her possessions, perhaps she found them in an opportunity shop, who knows. She was going around the dust car track of the van park, cabin to cabin. Asking if anyone would like to buy them. There was nothing fantastic about the furnishings, probably worth a hundred dollars or so. And she was only asking if anyone could spare ten dollars. And I don't even think this effort was for herself. I vaguely recall something about needing to put ten dollars into her daughter's bank account so the girl could afford to get on a bus and travel to Corinne's (there being some upset at the daughter's fathers where she was temporarily staying, an alcoholic with moods dependant on his cannabis consumption). I'll just note here that involved in this task of assisting her kid, Corinne would have to be humbled enough to scout out a buyer, and then walk or bus into town the ten kilometres to be able to deposit this small amount into her kid's bank account, and then most likely have to walk back to the van-village in the dark on the side of the road at dusk, as bus's were infrequent and stopped running in that direction mid-afternoons. Years later this is what people would recall about her. It was never too much trouble, if she could think up a way of a solution, and had the means of helping somebody. She wasn't a fool, or gullible, or had trouble being honest and refusing someone if she could do something for them. Corinne was simple, and she was a realist. Her simplistic honesty was undeniable.

The next few year's interactions were spotty. I remember some period where the girl of hers came to stay at the park. She barely graced Corinne's abode for a day before shaking up with some older male in a neighbouring van or cabin. Then later I remember Corinne telling me her girl had been evicted from the village by the managers, not being an actual renter, there was some argument somewhere and it was decided the non-paying party was the more suitable to go, vacate.

I remember Corinne telling me that she herself had given notice to management, soon after. Was due to leave the van park in a week or ten days, voluntarily. When I asked her why she told me that the rental rate was 85% of her pension income and so, by choice, she would find somewhere to pitch a tent. Maybe alongside the creek that ran its way from the other side of the cemetery, into and through the nearest town. Then, she explained, that all the money would be hers, hers to choose how to spend. She would then afford to eat what she wanted and be able to buy tobacco, but most importantly, have some money to give to her daughter, who was still suffering a constant struggle to secure permanent housing, (main expenses being pot and beverages). Theory behind this was if Corinne supplemented her then she in turn would be able to contribute to the supply of drinks, etc, to keep her 'landlord' of the week happy, thus delay arguments and subsequent impending evictions. I was dubious. I enquired whether this was ideal and was assured that she had given it a bit of thought, couldn't be swayed, it was not an impulsive decision making but an act of sacrifice and love.

 "That's what parents do, help their kids", this is what she said to me. I thought it was lunacy but given the logic presented, it wasn't really my place to dispute it, and I didn't want to embarrass her.

Life moves on, I had other distractions. I didn't see her again for a year or two, in 2015 I placed my boy into a day-care service, and began volunteering in a charity/opportunity shop in the town. I wasn't getting paid to work but I had to do something. The monotony and depressing atmosphere in the caravan park had me feeling suffocated and stagnant. My mood was much lifted when I kept myself active and useful. I felt the melancholy and despair of my immediate neighbours creeping in on me. To sit there every day was going NOWHERE, it wasn't living, a definite prelude back into alcoholism if I let it keep me. I volunteered at an organisation that also provided long term housing to low income applicants. The waiting list was long and unbeknown to me my situation had been noticed by some kind ladies in the church, which got me bumped up the priority list a little and within a year I was offered a long term tenancy in a gated community of apartments in town. This provided me with immense security that I hadn't been able to establish for myself previously. Once I moved into town, furnished our space with more than bed and cot, I was in a better position, transport wise, to begin attending meetings with a twelve step program. I needed to maintain the progress I had made so far. It was sitting in one of these meetings I encountered Corinne again. She reappeared to me in a different form, presenting another side of her.

 During our time as neighbours in the village van park, there was nothing about her that suggested that she had experience struggles with liquor in the past. She'd mentioned the occasional puff, but I had never actually seen her smoking. In normal Corinne form, I wouldn't have been surprised if she was pretending the pot was for her but the more likely scenario would be that anything Corinne ever managed to procure would be handed over to the young blonde daughter. I forget the girls name to be honest, although I can picture her in my mind, slight of frame, natural blonde, fine stringy hair. A lighter complexion than Corinne's earthy tan, not dark but some scattered freckles, brunette curly course hair and touch of olive skin, one would have to assume that the kid took after the father's colouring. But I don't know, I never saw him.

Corinne was not a group member of our fellowship, only attended sporadically, popping in for a cup of coffee and a Tim Tam biscuit. She never delved into specific details of her background story, preferring to philosophise and give out bits of positive cliché's, occasionally some sage advice. Our fellowship is an anonymous one so I'm loathe to go into a detailed account of her private past. What I can say is, like most of us in our groups, the common theme amongst us is and was a conscious gratitude expressed for having an improved mental state since being in charge of one's senses.

Time kept passing by, absorption in daily life, children, etc meant that I never really paid much attention to her or other regular characters around town. I never considered her a prominent feature in my world, not until now. That town had one central shopping centre and there were 'many' who frequented the area. Being inland from the beaches, the police used to round up all the transient and homeless people from the surrounding tourist areas on a seasonal basis. So pre-Christmas, Easter and school holidays, a lot of campers from the shores and National parks got pushed on from their regular parks and haunts along creek areas, to find refuge in our town. This resulted in up to 13 different charity or church services for the homeless. A men's shed, Le Shack ran by a retired pastor, a free hamburger night at the local railway station carpark, this sort of thing. Whereas most country towns or city suburbs usually only have two to four such services, that would provide grocery's, breakfast, a take-away hot meal, once a week hot showers, free toiletries, the occasional swag, donated tents or blankets, if you were lucky they'd score a sleeping bag, a change of clothes, female sanitary products, a hamper at Christmas, this type of stuff.

And the results of that... was an entire functioning social community of homeless people, visible to the rest of the town, undeniable in their presence. The park behind the Serviceman's Club was rife with people, making temporary shelter of the BBQ area's awning's, play forts and the little bridge that crossed over the creek that flowed through the park. The authorities knew about them, how could they not? But only bothered then when they became a bother. There have been acts of violence in the park, murders, overdoses, thefts. A lot of the time they dealt with each other in their own versions of justice. Only reaching out to police or ambulance if the situation became a fatality. No one likes a rotting body upwind of the tent now, do they? There was a kind of respect of each other, in a fashion, something akin to 'honour amongst thieves' or some empathetic acknowledgement of humility and compassion of like fellows.

Being a woman Corinne tended to avoid these hidden haunts. Corinne was durable, most certainly, but not a 'toughie'. Exhibiting her quiet common sense she kept herself visible, favouring the steps under the veranda on the side of the St Luce's Luthran church on Sydney Street, or the well-lit bus stop bench a block south of there, outside the million dollar cement construction of the Saving Army's church. Over the year's others camped there as well. Usually other females, or couples that wanted a veneer of safety.

I think Corinne may have tried having a tent site somewhere at some point. But preferably she favoured open areas. Desperation and poverty of fellow campsites proved to be a hazard, campsites were often pilfered by drug addicts, stand-overs, rough and tough bullies, necessity of misfortune.

Occasionally too, council workers did sweeps of lawn areas near bush land and council owned land and they mercilessly disposed of tents and property that was left unattended. I've heard complaints from more than one person saying that King Gee clad maintenance and groundsmen of the public works had bereft some vagrant of make-shift mattress, their few clothes, torches, buckets, whatever the poor souls few meagre possessions were.

Not a dummy, but prone to learn from survival, Corinne kept hold of her material possessions, first utilising a cheap black child's stroller to attach her bags and blankets. This little load was added to, and detracted from during the course of the next few years. Due to the element of the neighbourhood most people kept attentive watch over their items lest they lose them.

 There were occasions when I frequented the church, or was going by the taxi stand outside the shopping centre, and also at Saving Army's church where my fellowship meetings were held in a conference room, I'd see the unmistakable sight of a shopping trolley, loaded full of fabrics, clothing, miscellaneous bits and bobs, sometimes next to an empty coffee mug on the cement ground beside the trolley, usually the pram was there next to it also.

The afore mentioned 'street-people respect' came into play here. Any person eyeing off her trolley in hopes of salvaging some food or other prize, meaningless garbage to some, but gold to a person who has nil, was informed by any other persons nearby "Don't touch that, it's Corinne's". In her habitat of public view, Corinne earned herself a quiet reputation, a noted respect. She was never any trouble to any other person on the streets, kept to herself, absolutely did not get involved in any other person's business. I would wager she'd be the only person in the town's history who did not ever piss anybody else off. Her gentleness and generosity kept her in good stead with all who knew of her.

This leads me to write now about her interactions and associations at the Neighbourhood Centre at the bend of Jamies Street.

2016 and onwards became the time Corinne firmly connected herself to the community. Frequenting the Neighbourhood centre, where showers and a hot cuppa could be sought. Two small clusters of office rooms, connected by an open patio area housed a tea and coffee bar, refrigerator, tables and chairs, water cooler, notice board, an open wood slated veranda peeling off around the outer edges of the rear office rooms, a little laundry room and a disability toilet out back to the right, a meeting room off to the left.

I remember attending mother/child craft groups, and once a still-life drawing class in that back meeting room. A variety of community groups utilised the centre, occasional assistances like free legal or financial advice could be sought here on different days, men's support groups, holiday activities for kids. A table with free fruits and bakery items donated by local supermarkets.

Different versions of neighbourhood/community centres stud every little town across our country, all different, all pretty much the same. Volunteers, little old ladies man some, philanthropists and creatives. Corinne loved people. Loved to sit somewhere and have a chat. Despite her ordinariness she kept up her personal hygiene and never used her living circumstances as an excuse to be unclean, fashion was not a huge forte, but clean and tidy was something instilled from a young age. Common of the generation of her working class parent's decade, one didn't have to have the newest finest attire, but a clean pressed shirt and scrubbed face was paramount, anything less was unacceptable.

What I understand of her childhood was testament for this. Being an older sibling in a large family of kids, she was removed from school early, necessity being to care for the other offspring in order for the parents to be able to go to work. Corinne never formally completed even primary school, was for the most part illiterate, which limited her options when she herself came of employable age. An early marriage. A decade and society that placed low stock in a woman's education.

Kept down by societal dictations of only being useful enough to serve her duty as carer for others. Not fortunate enough I suppose to escape the back breaking jobs that some woman are forced by life and misfortune to acquire, fetching their forty to sixty percent of wages compared to men's pay rates despite doing equal works. No salvation of opportunity presents itself to these poor females, kept in shit by a patriarchal dependency. So like the majority, no career but mothering resulted.

The Centre.

This was information shared by the community workers and staff who spoke at her memorial. Part of Corinne's story that probably very few would have thought to ask about, people only being concerned mainly with themselves and all that...

Reminiscence's shared covered Corinne's fondness for sewing. The quirk being that she would peruse opportunity shops for a certain blouse, never holding out to uncover the style she actually wanted, always selecting an item that 'required' some slight alteration. Set up at the dining table in the middle of the Neighbourhood Centre, cuppa or glass of milk nearby, pull out her tiny sewing kit, making the necessary adjustments. Quite deft with a needle and thread. Not proudly, but just humbly set about altering a collar, sew up a pocket, place a dart in the back. Always refusing any invitation to take on someone else's alteration job, because her skills were noticed and noted upon by other patrons and staff alike. Contenting only herself.

Floral prints were the favourite. Funnily enough, once these personalised changes took place, it would be tried on, briefly modelled for a select one or two, taken off and gifted to another of the other people at the centre. A week later the scene would be repeated, another skirt or shirt sourced, repaired, given away. Yet another example of her humble nature, I don't believe the garments were ever intended for herself personally, but she was mindful of people's pride and would never infer the feeling of charity upon a person. Similarly, she'd never accept it from another, refusing all gifts and bestowments. And she had the art of giving, she'd throw out a comment about how she was 'throwing it away anyway', so the receiver was not made to feel obliged to her.

Over the course of her associations in the centre, Corinne would always be a willing participant in their publicity events, at one time she held up a large white cardboard poster which read "WOMAN OVER 55YRS FASTEST GROWING HOMELESS GROUP" in big bold red capital letters. Part of a campaign initiated by a social group for Homelessness Week, the story photographed and reported on in The Courier.

It is not a new revelation, when I googled this slogan I found similar reports made by The Financial Review, Housing For The Aged Group, Older Tenants Association, info @ property council, Marcy Foundation, Special Broadcasting Service (SBS), Australia Rights Commission, An Advertiser, Que Shelter, Church of Christians, a State Government report, House Older Woman Movement, Canada Geriatrics Journal, Democracy in government group, Mulgora Valley Gazette in September 2014, Ireland Business Service Organisation... the list is endless, I could fill the rest of the page with references, not just here at home, clearly this is a global issue.

On July 4th, 2021 residents of Nambour paid tribute to Corinne with all describing the Nambour Neighbourhood Centre volunteer as "the most lovely woman". Quoted her as "being the grandmother of the streets" in a report by N.Wynn in The Courier.

Followers of community groups on social media sites posted a memory on August 6th, 2021, "2 years ago with Corinne", for Homelessness Week 2021, with a photo of her holding up her poster from August 6th, 2019.

Again on July 16th, 2021, Nambour Neighbourhood Centre posted a copy of her memorial photo's, and she was mentioned again in their ANNUAL REPORT 2020-2021 where they "paid tribute to her generous nature and love of laundry by dedicating our community laundry space to her".

When I visited their website it states, "Our purposeful action is working to reduce the structural disadvantage that limits wellbeing and to provide a way up and a way forward for the most socially, culturally and economically disadvantaged and discriminated groups in our community".

A quick look at the program for Homelessness Week by HomelessnessAustralia.org.au shows availability of 'Supporter Pack's', a PDF containing information about 'meeting with your MP', how to download 'digital assets and posters', how to host a Homelessness Week event to support raising awareness of the issue.

I don't want to appear cynical but I have to wonder, how much was spent on creating these website's, doing research and typesetting, etc, to go into these 'awareness projects'? What is the result of them? Does being politically correct and 'making it a topic of conversation' actually do anything tangible? Did it help Corinne? If Corinne was so connected to these 'community supports' and her situation right there, in the faces daily of these 'helper's', then why did she sleep alone on a bus stop bench, for over a decade, middle of winter, finally succumbing to a hospital visit for her pneumonia, where she quietly and unfussily died, coincidently of a brain tumour, that ended her life, in the relative comfort and warmth of a hospital bed for that last night, just a day after her admission.

So, please, with sarcasm and scorn held back, please accept their invitation to 'join the campaign' at everybodyshome.com.au to support your advocacy with MP's...

Feel free to take heed of the event idea's :-

-invite people with lived experience of homelessness to a morning tea

-arrange an exhibition of art, photography, or other works

-run a forum or panel discussion

-host a breakfast morning tea or lunch for clients, workers, or the community

-organise an expo event bringing together various services and resources aimed to support people in need

-deliver a presentation to a school or a community group

-or, (and I love this one) host a conversation about home and why it's so important with people in your community, including those with lived experience of homelessness.

Better yet, do some physical good, donate what you can to providers like St V*ncent D* P**l, who house more people each year than the Queensland Housing department, or to B*ckp*ckBed-For homeless and read some ten shocking facts about homelessness at their website, the most vital to know is that social housing only accounts for 4% of all dwellings in Australia.

Https://theconversation.com/focus-on-managing-social-housing-waiting-lists-is-failing-low-income-households-120675

These organisations are willing to make your donation of a mere $2- tax deductable in Australia should you so require that!!

Okay, before we stray too far away from the story, I want to describe to you the personal quirks of Corinne, the things that people found endearing to her and elaborated on during her memorial service held by the Community Centre and personalised to her memorial. Corinne had a love for the colour blue. Blue irises, and blue lilly's were her favourite flowers, sometimes known as the Blue Lotus, the purple-blue flowers open from goblet shaped buds among the glossy, rounded lily pads. This tender waterlily is neat and compact so you can even grow it in a small pond or a water barrel on the patio, a botanical variety of Nymphaea nouchali. This flower befits her. I'm not sure if she knew of the symbolic relevance, but I feel apt to note it here. Given her penchant for regularly shaving her hair down to the shortest possible length and as soon as growth commenced she would dye her hair a dark blue. Hardly seemed worth the effort as Corinne would barely let her hair reach more than half a centimetre of growth before she would repeat the grooming process. Neighbourhood centre staff recalled fondly how she was forever dying and staining towels put out for use in the showers, with hair dyes of blue then would commit some ritual of bleaching them, something that no one really complained about, it was just a little joke.

During the memorial service guests were invited to share 'a glass of milk', being Corinne's favourite beverage. Volunteers mingled amongst mourners with wands of purple and blue semi-permanent hair dye and sprays and offered to create a lock of hair on each guest's head, to celebrate her passion for the hue. Small baskets holding pebbles and small flat river rocks were distributed, with gold, silver and coloured paint pens, allowing any who so wished to decorate a stone, to have as a keepsake, or to place in the stone garden that ran along the wall of the centre's driveway. I kept mine. I still have it.

The backyard between driveway side wall and the central covered patio was furnished with portable gazebo's and chair, all of the bench seats and office chairs were placed outside. Proudly I tell you that at least a third of the attendees were left standing.

Her eldest son, B. was the representative for the family, and was choked with emotion when he spoke. He informed us that a family funeral service had already been given, although when I watched a recording of that service I noted that it held none of the character of the scene at the tribute held in Nambour held several days after the family funded formal service, which was in comparison poorly attended in a funeral service hall, disappointingly impersonal, scripted, devoid of any colour or decoration. Only after that did B. learn of the Centre's intent to remember her, and up until his actual presence in the centre did he have any idea of the amount of people in Nambour who knew of and took the time to celebrate Corinne's life. No knowledge that she had come to be known, loved, remembered and included as one of their own people. He was genuinely surprised. I know that Corinne's illiteracy and refusal to own and operate a mobile phone would have been a factor in the lack of contact between them while she spent her days living on the streets. I was also not surprised to learn that she had not accepted his offers and attempts to find her accommodations in previous years. Corinne's daughter was not present at the memorial, sadly, or perhaps thankfully. But I know that she would be looking down at the assembled people that day and would have thought two things, "whatever is all this fuss about?", and that she was proud of her son, his young family and also of his occupation. He is a good man, who helps people, and did or rather does hold love for his mother.

Who knows what happens to people or how they end up where they do.

R.I.P Corinne, I miss you, you are not forgotten.

STUCK IN TODAY.

Friday

The view. The view is the weathered bandstand in the centre of Gympie's Memorial Park. A square but not a square with its charcoal brick base having 10 main pillars pushed out at the sides creating a hexagon-styled square, little benches pushing out at the sides. Whitewood latticed railings between each pole, barely supporting the top-heavy square roof reminiscent of a small house.

The old mildewed red brick-coloured roof tiles slant sharply up to give an impression of heights. Floodlights that may or may not still work are perched on top of each of the 4 sides of the roof given the yellowness of the glass in each light supports my theory that they may have stopped functioning many years past. An outdated style I suppose was intended to lend some importance or grand use in this park.

The entire construction is now fenced off, surrounded by scaffolding-type steel fencing, dotted with garish orange witches hats forbidding any park goers from climbing the 6 stout steps to enter the pitiful stand. The faded orange brick paving circling the stand appears to be sinking slightly on one side of it. This is highly probable given that this ground lies lower than the main street and was under a layer of flood water when I first sighted it in May when I moved here.

I arrived new to the town five days after a huge rainfall flooded the town and surrounding areas. It was an exciting long-awaited move North that was dampened by the 5 days I spent indoors, non-stop rain prevented me from exploring, and viewing Gympie and gave me pause to fully appreciate my top-floor unit in the higher side of the town. Everything was swamped then, as the Mary River raised itself up and spilled over onto the roads, cutting the town off from the Southside, and evaporating the majority of businesses operating on Mary St, the main CBD street.

Screeches puncture the faux peace here, white Galahs cover the ground in herds, having some meeting and then disappearing back into the tall trees, gone from sight but not unheard. A shrieking squall to frighten any other birds that might make a nice distraction.

The council have regenerated the shrubbery on my left at the edge of the park, little dome-shaped bushes that do not lend any prettiness or protection from the roadway that takes one from Mary St past the park and onto the M1, a highway whose noise is as unwelcome as the Galah's screams.

Once a gold mining town I'm sure this large, grassed area was used as a welcome and festive place, however, on this clouded afternoon my line-of-sight fights with noisy cars and the cemented carpark areas at the rear of banks, meat market, the dollar-shop and real estates.

Yet this is the nicest spot nearby to my home that supplies me with a table and bench, some sunlight, fresh air and most of all the simplicity of just being outside. Clouds creep over, a cool afternoon following three days of a brutal heatwave. Today is Friday and I've been to the dentist this morning. Surprisingly without horror nor pain. My dentist has given new meaning to his profession, a gentle and lovely young man, who has changed my horrible opinions of dentists as butchers, the stuff of waking nightmares.

Today was the last required appointment that has been happening in a weekly series for the past month. A change in employment afforded me to attend to some maintenance long overdue, not hardly as awful as I had expected. It is a strange sort of satisfaction that I suppose comes to one of my age, to be able to manage one's functioning body parts. Forcibly coaching me to admit to myself that all is not done with as of yet, some maintenance is in order and making me realise that it is needed and that yes, indeed I'm only part-way through, and more living is yet to be done.

I marvel at the thought, no, I am not young, but what I thought would be the end game is only perhaps midway. I won't use the word wisdom perhaps it's a maturity, acknowledging that I may have to create some life, some 'things-to-do' to fill up the gap between 50 and 80 or so. I had not considered that to be a possibility, and so here I am. An alien to pursuits, I must laugh, as I lift my head and observe myself alone in a somewhat empty park. But I'm only here to please myself so it shall have to do!!

Raindrops threaten. I am in no rush to leave here. The breeze is refreshing. I pause for a cigarette and to assess the sky.

Anyway, I've noted my most recent favourite author is Virginia Woolf. I did begin with some curiosity about her, having heard vague reference's during my life, I think a line in some movie, 'Who's afraid of Virginia Woolf'. And not understanding the reference other than she was a feminist that some unenlightened men would tease each other about.

Then I saw a movie called Orlando on SBS world movies so when I perused the classics section of the local Gympie Library, I pulled her title from the shelves, not knowing what I would read, and it turned out to be a collection of her essays. Which I admit I found curious but was forcing myself to halfway through and retired it. Not for lack of understanding as the theme was very evident but repeated.

Having got the message, I returned it a week later, then another of her titles was suggested to me by the librarian's search and I am currently enthralled with 'The Waves'. It is fabulous and the inspiration has come to finally pick up my pen again, fill a drink bottle and set up in the park, cigarettes in hand and buy a notepad on the way. Secondly, I like the writer John Steinbeck, whom I am equally enthralled by at this point, I had read 'The Grapes of Wrath' months ago, then searched out seven or eight of his other titles. In my librarian's search, I was also presented with "Mad at the World, A life of John Steinbeck'. Just as interesting as his novels.

Not having any formal training in literature as they do, I do not feel deterred. Nor do I feel that I have any particular style or format. I simply feel that everyone has at least one interesting story, or not, but it is in the descriptive words that could captivate or entertain a reader. So, I go forth, not knowing how to do it just that for me it must be done.

It is 4 o'clock in the afternoon, the cars on the roads surrounding me and the motion around the park is slowing down, not as noisy, not as hurried, and the raindrops are holding off as yet. Not threatening anymore, just a grey smoky glare overhead in the sky.

I will walk home now, as nothing is a given. Yesterday's flash storm is an example of the 32-degree heat and the fan pumping night and day in my flat when I suddenly heard a clunking on the tin and looked out the front door to see hail hitting the stairwell and lawn. So, I'll return home now satisfied that I have started. I'll mention here that 'home' is going to be another description entirely.

Saturday Morning

At home.

I wake at an early hour as usual. This is a result of my going to bed earlier and earlier. A late night is 9.30 PM. But I start to tire by 7, forcing myself to stay out of my bed until 8:30 PM. This I try. It's not so much I am exhausted from vigorous days but more that in this place I have learned that sleep is valuable, and

I should take the quiet times to my advantage. The neighbours are unpredictable in their sleeping routine, not minding the fellows next door when they want to pump up the volume of their music. Also, the visitors are many. Calling out from the carpark as they arrive. Repeatedly calling out the names of the residents they seek. Knocking loudly and over and over, despite the indication that the persons they want may appear not to be home. It might be different if I had only one neighbour on each side of me.

However, it is not a house it is a unit block and the people sought far outweigh me in number, myself being only one. There are 14 units in this block. With 30-odd residents inside the walls. The number varies, greatly, changing all the time. Not a problem of overcrowding but rather a flow and ebb of changing people/ homeless, friends (cough-cough), and some acquaintances who will soon outlive their welcome and move on.

Also, some who live on the outside of the walls. That's right, a young indigenous man with no shoes is a constant figure in the yard, in the carpark, and on my stairwell. It used to bother me. To describe it would be to say that an unwashed, mute man lurks outside my door. But after some months of passing him every time I go outside, I must say that he is calm and not a bother.

It's simply his presence that disturbed me. Not his actions. Months ago, I assumed he suffered a type of disability, mentally, but now we greet 'good morning', and 'hello', as we pass. I've never seen him enter another flat. Never seen him talking to any other tenants. I am not sure which flat he may actually be attached to. Every few weeks he may appear to have changed his outfit. Always standing. Never once have I seen him sitting. Many visitors pass through these grounds, coming and going. Never speaking to him and now I find his being there is quite normal. His withdrawn and silent behaviour is, I feel now, a familiar constant.

 Something is comforting about familiar content. I don't know his name. I've never asked. I won't, I no longer feel any threat by his existence, pacing (more strolling) in the carpark, circling the mailboxes, silently viewing the rubbish bins, the gutter, and the sky. There absolutely has to be something going on there. Some dysfunction of the social skills. I'm guessing it's more likely a sad result of his experience in this world. A product of his prior and present environment. I have already sighted and greeted him this morning. A half hour ago when I made tea and bagged up my recycling. Taking it down the stairs to the fenced-in garbage bin area at 7 AM and there he was, we said hello, and now below me I hear his bare feet stepping on the cemented carpark. Looping around the side wall, stopping where the wooden fence and backyards meet the neighbouring wall and slowly turning, creating yet another lap, slowly, gently, boringly. This is the limitation of his adventures.

Today I have decided I think to ask him his name next time I pass him. Of course, by then I may forget this resolution in the course of going about my day's activities. I also may not, as I do not encourage friends or visitors here. The air is cool this morning. Pleasant. The sky is the bright light that is barely a colour. I think it is a shade of white one might find on a paint sample card at the hardware store. A variation of glaring white, not realising it has other tones until placed next to another sample card of the purest white. It hurts to stare out my balcony at it. It is a beautiful temperature.

Yesterday I unplugged my television and moved it from my lounge room and set it up on top of a wardrobe in my bedroom. A further attempt to recede into a quiet space. Secluding myself from the interest of any other residents or their visitors. My dark curtains are always kept drawn in the front rooms. Black cotton covers the small window in my little kitchen and along the same front wall is a navy-blue heavy curtain, preventing people from seeing their way into my lounge room. These windows face the south side of the flats where a cement stairwell and landing have all the traffic. Not cars. I mean people's foot traffic. Erratic but constant flow of rude, noisy, drug addicts. Drunken people.

As one who indulged for the better part of my adult years, I have no snobbery when I describe these peace intruders as definitely the lower class. They do not like anyone here. Not visiting friends. They come to destroy themselves, and also my peace and quiet. They seek out any one of the number of drug dealers here. There are a few.

I am in the minority. A mature single woman. I stay quiet. I keep to myself. I do not make friends. I do not invite guests. Do not keep my front door open for fresh air. Do not allow anyone inside, draw attention, get involved, ask questions or shop too much. I keep my furnishings simple, second-hand, and I don't play music. I keep to myself.

This is a place where you bear the loud music, stay inside when you hear yelling, don't answer questions, and don't make a fuss. Just go about my business in quiet. Not rousing interest, avoiding the front landing and path when groups of visitors are out there, for fear that one day one of the traffic will be recognised as someone who knew me in a former life in another town. Not too far away. Close enough. It frightens me. I do my best to stay in my own orbit. I have no desire to reengage with anyone that I knew before. That's why I moved here. To start anew.

I'm not actively hiding, just trying to regain some peace in a reconstructed life. My life has crashed and burned but I did not go with it. I'm still breathing. So, I had to relocate because dysfunction surrounded me and refused to let me go. I went and I'm glad. It's all so calmer now. All the cliché's of 'everything happens for a reason' vein appear to be true. I may not have grown into who I now am had I not endured what come before. God dammit, I am getting older and wiser, hindsight and all that. Further proof that my life will go on for its second half-century.

Wait, I don't wish to lose track. I'm attempting to describe my home now, not fully my home, but rather the place where I reside now.

How does one give an accurate description of it, for the feel, the character, the meaning (or lack of) of it?

A cool breeze comes in and flows thru the open glass sliding doors on my balcony, to the right side of my bed. I have the TV on my left. I lay face down, pen to the page. I am happy and calm. Content that this new project occupies my thought, in a way that doesn't keep me monitoring the time passing.

The balcony is little, 90cm deep and, 2 meters wide. It is enough. I have a latticed panel of dark green zip-tied to the railing, covering the open space at eye level. Obscuring the view in, deterring any intruder and, keeping people out; there is a wooden blue armoire, vintage, full of fishing and camping equipment. Stored away, no use now. Not used since I moved in. I miss fishing. This pursuit is postponed until April when I'll get my driving licence back. I moved here from the beaches near Kawana, Queensland. Fishing was my main go-to there, while I waited for my housing. It was an economical past time.

And a wooden hutch or buffet posed as my bench seat. A doddery clothesline pulls out from the wall. Attaches to the other side. Never functions properly, always makes my clothes fall to the ground. Silver metal and grey ceramic pots for plants. Jade and geranium cuttings I pilfer from yards on my way home, walking uphill from the shops two blocks away. Seven or nine pot plants now. Growing nicely. The daily watering is my homage, pretending that I still nurture living things in my home. Now, I do not. My children are gone, the loves departed, the betrayers evicted and lost, no longer posing as my friends.

This space does not allow for a pet, I never liked the commitment of pets, not once the children were gone.

The ending of a movie about Darwin is on the TV. I go to the kitchen and microwave some rolled oats with brown sugar and milk. I return to my bedroom. I eat with a spoon, standing up.

A lawn mower drones outside the balcony, or a wiper snipper. Yes, a cutter, starting and stopping. Taking advantage of this cool sweet air, before any heat comes of the day, a French film begins, is in sub-titles but I'm not watching it anyway. I just like the sound of words in my background. I don't need to understand the works, but it fills my space with something other than the reminder that I am alone. I wash my hands. The cutter stops. The novel 'The Waves' sits next to me on the bed, quietly waiting to deliver some more inspiration for my writing, in case the flow of this stops.

Factually, my description of home has not even begun. This little flat. Cream-painted brick interior, two rooms, with an open kitchen separated from the lounge by a half wall come bench just 1.2m high and a metre wide, to give the impression of it being another room, or more so to give an edge to the sink which is placed below the window. A shower room completes the forth corner and doubles as a laundry. Oh, and a closet, with a water heater in it.

Curious now, I go to the balcony pulling a measuring tape from a milk crate of tools 4 metres wide by 8 metres long.

This is the space. The entire space in which I live.

Alone. Oh, how the mighty have fallen.

But I'm inside. It is clean, it functions, and for now, it's mine.

This is what the government housing has allocated to me, following a year and a half in temporary accommodation unit in Kawana, Queensland.

I am one of the homeless, stuck in a housing crisis that evolved during the Covid epidemic, displacing a lot of families. I was suffering my own disaster when Covid restrictions began in Australia at the beginning of 2020. My full house collapsed, the children taken, and my life ended. Friends gone. I'll pause here, Virginia Woolf is calling me.

I go to the kitchen. I pour more hot water into my reused teabag of herbal flakes. I must shop but I have already spent an amount this week. My savings are taking a blow. It was an investment really. Healing myself. An investment in the well-being of my future living. This dentist is not cheap. Long delayed and avoided, so I guess that it's an overdue spending. Something other people do properly, or others do not at all. I am satisfied. At the same time aware that such expenditures cannot be continued in any more frivolous way.

Necessities must be had, I recently saved $3,000.00 and poured two of that into the upkeep of my person. Fixing this and that. I should remain careful now. My employment is not lasting. I was lucky to find the last job, a rare thing for me. Legal gains. This week my employer told me that I shall not be needed any further during December. Not for a month, until the Christmas holiday is finished.

So, December will be no definite income and January will resume it again. It doesn't frighten me. I have enough. I'll visit my parents before Christmas Day, where my daughter lives. That will be the majority of the expenses, for the others that seek to control me have indicated that they won't allow me to visit my sons. There are no reasons given. They just like to be viscous, my punishment for their pleasure.

That is the emptiness of it really. The need for creativity. For projects. To occupy my time. To detract the pain from my mind.

The mowers stop.

They restart. How many lawns are about me anyway?

The music comes loudly as I lay to read. They are intuitive. They sense when I want silence.

I turn off my TV. My background noise. Country music is the closest neighbour's selection this morning.

Door's slam. Voices. Mowers stop.

The heat is beginning. The sky is still brilliant ash white. Cars go faintly up to the road out front. Saturday is beginning. It is 9.30 am, I feel restless. I feel exhausted. This is the trouble of it. My sensible head knows that I should go out! Exercise. Go to the gym located in the local pools Gympie Aquatic Centre. I should walk there early before the heat. Before my day progresses and I find some reason not to go. I can go later anyway. It is the weekly routine of some of my acquaintances to go on Saturday afternoons, before our afternoon meeting in the halls on Stanley Street.

I have already texted and said I am not going today. I still have time to change my mind. It's the stubbornness in me that made me send that cancellation. It's the regular routine to swim with some members of my fellowship every second day during the week. But after joining them for a few weeks now, I revolt. It is now assumed that I am to be a constant attendee, and on days that I have not agreed to go, one of them will arrive in my car park to pick me up. I resist this, I will not be directed. I'll go when I say that I am going. Yes, I know it is stubbornness. I am aware of that. I resist being herded.

A disadvantage of not having my driver's license is of letting people into my life when I require help with something or to go somewhere. It feels too controlling. The explanation is that my fellowship has four weekly meetings and when I should choose not to attend there is often a question as to why. I will not be beholden to anyone else's expectations.

There is no onus on me to go. I am not required to attend. I go because I want to and for example, if I have worked a tiring and sweaty day then I reserve the right to skip an odd meeting. No harm in it. Most of the other members go to only one night a week of their choice. That is their routine. However, I have been frequenting all four meetings and should I not adhere to all some other member sends me texts asking, "Are you okay?". A bit short-sighted and indulgent of them. I will not be bullied. It takes all the joy from it. Attending because someone else thinks that I should. That is not the point of it. I will resist these people. Probably well-meaning but nevertheless they ruin the entire event for me.

I do not need to be coaxed. I know what I am doing.

Have I given away something here? It is maybe some insight to you that gives away why I act that way.

I don't care. Stop thinking about me.

I live for me, not for you.

How I detest expectations. They are heavy and I don't want more friends. Any friends. It is inconvenient for me.

I want to sleep. I know that I'll just lay there. My mind will keep hurtling on, till I have to rise because I'm just making myself unhappy in my mind.

Book to the side. Sorry Virginia I want to hear you. I do. Too many distractions. I don't like weekend days in Gympie. Half-day Saturdays. Forcing me to make my decisions regarding outings early in the day. Before I am ready. Or else I must wait. All through Sunday when nothing happens.

But nothing is happening, here, now, alone in my room. Nothing except what is in my mind, racing. This is the current way that time makes me. It's endless. Ongoing. Awake in my mind. The ultimate hypocrisy is that I don't want people in my life, I want to be without them, but I do struggle with being alone. I know why, it's the people, the people I can fill my hours with are simply not the ones that I want. No more substantial. No less precious in the eyes of God. It angers me, I want my people. My children, the family that I created, and without them there will be no acceptable substitutes. I am just here. Awake. Alive. Oh, I'm becoming morose. A change of location is a temporarily fix, I must go outside. The walls of my unit are once again suffocating me. Or my mind. Another hypocrisy is that my safe place, my sanctity is what I think is smothering to me now.

Toast. Tuna. Margarine.

Getting up to prepare it. This is what rescues me. Being functional. I function. I do what is needed. I live. I shall walk. Reset.

When all of this – desire and joy and pain – has melted away and dissolved in stormy rapture.

And then refreshed itself in blissful sleep, you will revive, revive to fullest youth.

To fear, to hope and to desire once more.

- John Wolfgang Von Goethe

Okay, I have shaken myself out of it.

I did lie down. My mind whirled. My mind was not as exhausted as my body was pretending to be. Who, I ask, has generally exhausted themselves by 10 o'clock in the morning by doing nothing more than just waking and being in existence.

I made the toast. I prepared my handbag, putting in the two short novels ready to return.

The Kindness cup by Thea Astley

The Pearl by John Steinbeck

There is always a selection of borrowed books in my house. Some waiting for me and some that are finished.

I made some cinnamon bread, stirred the mixture in a metal bowl and added the warm milk. Covered it with a tea towel and left it to rise up on my stove in its bowl. Not a warm place, as instructed, but enough. Room temperature will suffice as it will sit there for longer than the prescribed hour, I don my black sunglasses, and lock my front door. Pad in the bag. Pens in the bag. Some coins, my mobile phone and a credit card, lest I require more distractions before I return to my home.

The sky now has shape soft grey clouds sitting thick, but light perched in front of the white glare behind. Two raindrops touched my arm. Barely. In hesitation. Not threatening but not declining.

Yes, I did pass the shoeless man, out the front of the units. I did weigh my options on whether to ask him his name. I think it was a nice thought, me pretending that I am going to be social. It didn't happen. He must be intuitive. Behind my dark glasses, impenetrable to the sight of others I watched him walk toward me, not 'to' me, past me. I stayed impenitent. He turned his head away allowing me to remain resolute. Unbothered. Unfriendly. Unharassed. A solitaire. He is like me. Sombre.

The pavement is grey and quiet as I pass the school, as you would expect on a Saturday. Crossing the hilled street, into the leafy pass. Slopes downhill into the park, slants too great to go straight across on foot. Have to cling to the edges and track around.

Refreshed, books returned. Stock replenished. Library closing. It is noon.

I go back home revived. How did I get from 9:30 AM to noon? My mind nags me.

McLeod St Park.

Poinciana's, Jacarandas. Greyer puffs, I pretend there is a sun. Birds call, not sharply, sweet, chattier. The great, great tree beside me covers most of the area. Bigger than my home, at the least two-thirds of my entire unit block. Timeless. Great. Must be a hundred years old at the minimum, still healthily going strong. Again the space is empty. I am the only person enjoying the park, set beside the library. Two picnic tables with benches. A water fountain for drinking, not the sort for decoration. Unused exercise equipment on the other sides of the grass grounds. No people. Peace. Many smaller birds enjoy their conversations. No people. No one is evident in their front yards. Houses line up across the road on the further side of the park, what is with this place? A taxi drives by. Is it sleepy? This country town.

This rural city is in between the Sunshine Coast and the Moreton Bay Areas. These street-side houses have cultivated gardens, mowed lawns, and all weather-boarded Queenslanders with awnings over the windows and solar panels atop the roof. Frangipani's rule. There is a bus stop over there. Two houses within ten metres of me are boasting flagpoles. Australia's flag dances proudly. Another car goes up the street. It doesn't stop.

 The wind is light. Beautiful. Just right. The grey clouds fade into the glare of the background white.

Where are the people? I know that they inhabit here. I see cars in the driveway's carports and garage spaces. I hear no voices, no children playing, no shouts. An ant crawls across my notepad. Behind me is the David Nimmo Centre, the local Meals on Wheels. I guess they don't work on the weekends. Beyond that is another climb going up yet another hill. Some lazy stores on the left bend. Goes past a blind store, paint store, antique dealer, and barbershop.

All are closed on a Saturday afternoon.

I could walk on, another mile. Seek out some life at the café. Cross the bridge and tracks to the Mary Valley Rattler, a historical train platform. Rusty Rails café. Vintage trains perform tours with nostalgia. A money spin. Overpriced, senior citizen friendly. I worked there in the kitchen for a month when I arrived here in May. They have a lot of volunteers and are a tight group. So friendly to their guests, but the economy ruling their way. Suzi the cook. Proud. Works hard. Bess, the tiny lady fiercely protecting her position and way. Train drivers who love their job, dream job. Easy. Fun. Enviable.

Some cars pull up at the park. I leave here.

Gentle, sloping upwards, the hilltop of my home. I punch the bread down. Place it in a tray. Reheat some lamb and carrot stew.

No shoe's is out there. Where does he go when it rains? Silly question. He will still be out there.

The lounge room is a different space now. Now without the television in it. Better. Larger. No distraction from its true purpose.

It holds three small vintage cupboards, wooden, one pink, one gold and one varnished. A coffee table. The couch dragged from the offices of my former address in Kawana. A gift from the manager, who arranged this new residence for me. Allocated me my lot.

A church man. A helper. Dave.

He paid for my refrigerator, my washer and my microwave. As I left, he told me his mission, to outfit me so I would never need to be homeless again.

The living it part is up to me.

13 collected wall crucifixes, all adhered to the dividing wall between the lounge and bedroom. They sit in my view. Placed deliberately above my head as I pass from room to room and back again. Dishes. Lamps. Standard additions.

It is different to everyone else's unit in this block. I have created it as my own. I create in it.

Explanation- the cupboards house my art supplies. My craft tools, paints, brushes, glues, stencils, pencils, crayons, media, materials, papers, rulers and tools.

Every week in Kawana I collected these things. I knew that I would get here in my place, my own space.

I knew what I would make here, and I have. I am.

Removing the T.V. to the other room has created an increased work space. More to place my works in progress. With my unfinished works and my ideas forming. I will buy a dining table this week. It will be my raised working space. So far, I have been using my floor, covered with a canvas tarp and mean on my back. It is a small room. But I will make do here. It is a step in my recipe, for I have a bigger picture of my life brewing. This will do for now.

Sunday Morning

I won't re-read what I put down yesterday. No need to look backwards to the dimness. The afternoon was exceptionally better., a short nap. A quick descent of the hill. Stopping at the supermarket proved to be a battle. I do understand that I have some people who are well-meaning and care for me. It just seems people like it better when I have some problem. I know a lady Jean, a feisty 85-year-old. Not ready to throw in the towel. Outgoing in her care and concerns. I think the lady (yes, she is a lady) will gather any remnant of an excuse to express her concerns and tell me that I can always go to her.

Should I have any issues. No one else can fix my issues, I shouldn't want them to. They are mine. Exclusively mine. It's all well and good to offer assistance but it's all mute if nothing can be done. I don't need someone to console me. I'm always talking to myself anyhow.

So, the battle has begun, I sight them as I'm entering the shopping complex. I wave. Acknowledge that I'm still a friend. Yes, yes.

Yes, I've seen you. Glad you're well, on I hurry. No, not enough, she would follow me. Goodness! I turn back as I round another corner, I know she's following me now. Her husband totters along behind her. He is more like me. Happy to wave, smile, and continue on with his business. I call out that I can't stop, I am late.

Jean does not give in. She is chasing me down. Ohhhh. I have to stop. She is old. It aggravates me. I tell her I'm fine. I reassure her. I admonish her. I repeat myself. It is tiring. I inform them that yes, THANK YOU, I am now late. I didn't have time to stop and chat. This aggravating explanation steals precious minutes from me. Now I am pissed off. Now they are appeased because I need them, great!! Furious, I insist they drive me and drop me off to where I was headed because, yes, now I am bloody late, late!

I arrive at my fellowship meeting in the church hall on Stanley Street. It has begun. I move quietly like a thief to the closest empty chair in the back row. I don't go and sit with my friends. I don't want to receive their approval nods and smiles. Yes, she is here, good, approval, smugness.

I go for me, for myself. Not for the old timers that feel their duties are fulfilled if they have been encouraged on more to the fold.

My encouragement is within myself. I own it. I shall administer it.

I really do enjoy the meetings more if I'm in my own tent, my own bubble. I resist being herded.

I could have called anyone of 9-10 people I know who were there and asked them to pick me up. Give me a lift to save the hills. I don't like to make plans in advance, be committed. Herded. Obliged. Obligated. I want to option of seeing how I'm feeling just before the time. Besides I need the exercise. I'm steadily growing bigger. I am now heavier than I have ever been in my life. Even when pregnant. When I've been with child I could wear a jacket and people would not even guess that I was carrying.

So, I enjoy the meeting, listening to the speakers, give their testimonies. The chair of the meeting spots me and jots down my name on his attendee book. I signal with a hand gesture and a mock frown. He smiles. he knows I don't like being called upon for my testimony every week and not today when my lovely dress is no longer lovely, it has passed its usefulness. I'm too fat now for this cut. I grimaced when I pass a glass shop front window half an hour before.

Too late to go home and change. Already late. I must get a full-length mirror installed in my flat. Seriously need to avoid these tragedies. I look awful. Old lady arms. Tattoo's no longer look cool on these pudgy limbs. Just wrong. My gut is not low, it is round, it is unignorable.

I sit in my seat with my handbag over my stomach. I know it's in vain, it won't really hide a thing. But I cannot stay sitting any other way. I'm the only person in the rear row. I suffer a wave of humiliation when I swing my foot in my chair. This catches the corner of an eye of a fellow sitting diagonally in the row in front of me. He is large too. He gets it. Doesn't even do a full turn. Doesn't find me worth appraising. Pretends he hasn't seen me. I am glad. I'm too awful to be seen. The bowl passes. We put in our coins. We pray, I lift my chair from its row and stack it along the sides of the walls of the hall. We mimic each other.

I do know that one member is departing the township this week and I see him across the room of moving people. I creep through. Greet him, supply my email. Congratulate quickly and enquire to him. A genuine young man. Gareth. I think he's going to make it. I pray his return to Canberra goes well. He has my email if he returns here anyway. It's all I can do.

An interruption. A tap on the shoulder. Jesus Christ. There is no escape. A dinner request. I don't want to go. I am fat and have already eaten. But I accept with sarcasm. "I am not paying." The old man smiles. Can they sense my aggravation? I'm sure they enjoy it. I want to steer my own course. Does he think that I am flirting? No, of course not, I am their work, his prodigy.

I go. I refuse to sit at his end of the table, I solidly place myself on the other side of Lane, an old friend. A no-nonsense woman. She will buffer me.

I practice conversation, I use the pauses to not do conversation. Food arrives, not what I asked for.

Does he think he is gracing me by adding things onto my plate, I am aggravated and say it aloud. This is not what I ordered. Lane rescue's me and asks me for the offending salad. She is deft. She is practised. She saves Nevil's honour. Someone will eat the salad. I have been sufficiently buffered, from the conversation and the focus. I smile. I leave early. I am mentally lighter and happy to go. Some distraction has been had. It has taken me out of myself. I sleep early.

Sunday

I woke refreshed, it is still cool. The clouds are white and many, not as patched with grey cotton balls like yesterday, there are a few slight patches of light blue.

These remove a lot of the blinding glare. The breeze is up. I smell blossoms. Summer is in town.

I'll go with this feeling, a motivation, it is the day with nothing in it to do, Sunday. I will use this empty day and put the shame of my fat into my motivation. I will pack a bag and a towel. I will join a membership at the Aquatic Centre, with the Gym. Today is the day. I must get on with it, any bigger and the sadness will kill me. Will be unliveable. I will write. I will swim. I will exercise. I am outside.

Okay. I have arrived. A slow walk across town with my backpack. I pause and sit at a picnic table atop the historic railway station. I got down the activities of the evening before. I sit at the unused end. Away from the café goers and train enthusiasts. Out of view of the busy staff. I don't seek out my former workmates. I don't greet. I seek solitude. This intermission in my walk is perfect peace. I had passed already the Suma Suma Café, alive and gay with the custom of the cheery Sunday morning.

I considered a stop-in for half a moment, knowing it wasn't a full thought to be met with any actual decision. I had intended to walk through the underground railway tunnel, up the stairs and jump off the platform in an automatic fashion. I saw the platform table and halted there, a pen from my backpack. Cigarette from the packet. I feel relieved as I put down a few pages. Is it progression? Is it purging?

Travis, a train tour conductor passes me, treading past me to inspect an old carriage, now used to store unengaged café furniture. Seasonal decorations, other business junk.

He smiles hello, and greets me, no other conversation is required. He goes about his business. A train fanatic. An enthusiast. If I'm not working on the train today, then he has no interest in speaking to me. I am no longer a contributor. I am happy with this. Satisfied to be left on my own, in peace. I wish for no distraction from writing out my notes. Do not seek to entertain any enquiry as to why I'm there. I do not assume to disturb others. My aura is select.

Pad returned to carry-all, wander to the steps, descend onto the carpark, depart history and sandwich's made.

Cross the wide old open street.

Party supply store. Supplement store; The Real Body Movement.

Savers Product and Garden Centre are all closed.

The Men's Shed on my left. Curiosity sale on my left. All closed.

The Two of Us Café, none of them are there today.

Further on, an open door.

Now, this interests me.

Timeless Treasures second-hand, vintage, used furniture store.

Wide front, barn-size doors open, and the trademark vintage child-size tricycle decorate the entrance to the middle door. I like this, I am enticed.,

I know I won't buy anything today. My mission is another thing, planned out already. Pleasant (pleasing) curiosity pulls me inside. Interesting wooden furniture, curio cabinets, artist tables, knick knacks or spice display shelves are intent on being mounted and cheap. No gluttony here. Realistic people-friendly prices.

The expected China. A modern jewellery display cabinet. A glassed locked box. Many linked rooms, an open, large-spaced tour of a building that I think was definitely at one point a house.

Most friendly lady. Not pressing. Just the right amount of talking.

Italian chaise lounge sets, topaz velvet, polished wood. Already sold. Mandatory antique farming tools, meat mincer, hand cranked. Landscapes on walls, guild frames, marble-edged mirrors, beauty, a file to store in my memory. A vendor I'll gladly return to once I have a home big enough to receive such grand items. Not a junk store. Indeed, some are named timeless treasures. Farewell. I meant it. Good day to you.

Around the right corner one more park. I stay on the footpath. Lush greenery. Thickened grass. Bare of people, far-flung swing set, not islands of table and chairs. Lacking invitations of sitting. This is a picnic blanket space. A shame. It's lovely. The tallest tree's above my head, I pass under them on the sidewalk.

Pass by Nevil's house on my left on the other side of the street, his van is there, with open doors in the driveway. No need to stop by, that is a personal place. Too familiar, it would be for me to encroach there. I see him several times a week, five days or more I either work with Nevil, attend the same fellowship meetings and swim at the Aquatic Centre with him and others. I accept lifts, transport, and dinner invitations, all friendly enough however I have reached the barrier, the boundary where too much familiarity would be uncomfortable for me. I feel the necessity to reverse the helpful invitations, guarding that ledge of mine that demands of independence, how fucking awful to seem incapable. This I how the elder members of the fellowship get to you. Helpful, ever helpful. Without guarded caution one becomes entranced. Trapped. Obliged. Even if that is not the intent of the helper it always turns out this way. I suffer very repellent feelings when it comes to accepting help from others.

3 houses past Nevil's, the park footpath ends. I cross over to his house's side. I am at the pools.

Newly constructed. Modern steel art installations are perched in the grass before the entrance. Stainless steel curved pole's, stuck together, linear, imitating bends of waves.

Flocks of Corella's rear about in a repeated circle formation above our head. Tempted by the water, a tease, for the landing is not ideal, the space on the ground overtaken by moving children. Loudly squawking. Deterred by flesh-limbed loudness covered by neon bright Lycra and spandex costumes. Children at play. Enjoy. Squeals of delight. Mild directions are given by parents and minders. Calling each other names, join my fun, watch me enjoy myself.

This is where the people are. The Gympie population. I attend this venue during the weekdays, but the patron is different, midweek are the seniors, the older community, refusing to retire. Fighting to stay active, remain able. Give themselves an activity. A reprieve from doilied tables and gout, arthritis and injury. Physiotherapy of bodies and of life. The grey-haired set that refuses to give in, the same one I'm suffering from. It's not an insult. No judgement here from me. I give recognition of the malady. I too am affected. I am older than my age, not that I imagined that I would get here. Never knew that I would here arrive, coming too early just the same.

I am making the commitment to my body, a delayed financial commitment, a membership, and a plastic keyring token that shall pass me automatically thru the silver metal poles that form the glass panels, that make up the entrance/exit barrier gates. I am part of it now. We are one. For the past 2 months, I have accepted the invitation to swim. Joined Nevil and Kriz at their bi-daily sessions.

I was reluctant to commit. Paying per visit, and unsure if I would accompany them next time, or next week. This is one of my resistance actions, I didn't want to sign-up for a weekly debit from my bank account funds unless it was proven to be a value. Hesitant to have another wasteful expense.

I was kidding myself. Triumphant in ensuring that the decision was mine alone, not impulsive and regretted, not directed or for the approval of any peers. The guy's routine was an acceptable introduction. The staff recognised me as a local regular now. I am familiar with the geography and know my way around the facilities. The few fellow lady swimmers introduced their names to me. I am not shunned. Am accepted for my size. It is not uncommon. We, ladies, recognise our equalness in each other.

Yes, I'm here because I'm fat. I'm here to slow my dying. Yes, I live alone, and yes, you may greet me anonymously, but do not come too close. Yes, we are all here together. Your proximity affords me the company needed; your conversation is not sought. A nod. A smile. Just keep walking past me. Yes, some sunscreen. Yes, a coffee. No, no need for your number, I will not call you. You are friendly, you are not my friend. I will see you here. That is enough. I thank you.

Hair is permitted to be messy here. Cellulite dimples are allowed. It is a rare place that allows people to just be who they are in all their flaws.

Reminder's that we are Australian here. Surf brands. Ripcurl, Billabong, Zoggs. Families, chicken nuggets, chips. I love our present culture.

A squawking black crow. A pair of pigeons brave the edge of the tiles and touch their feet to the cooling water flowing over the lip of the tiles. Smart flyer's, the pair won't stop their necks to drink. Pearl grey intelligence. Know that chlorine is not nice to drink.

Neon orange. Babbled chatter. Dripping tendrils. Sunhats. Cans of Solo soft drink. Raiders t-shirts. A squeal.

Black cotton, blue Lycra, and lifeguards in alarming contrast of Red and Yellow.

Whistles on cords around necks, straw hats, life preservers. Sunblock appointed. On guard. Youthful. Ever ready. Trusted, sneakers on, hand-held radios attached to hips.

Peter's ice creams, goggles, pies. Family members of another race throng through the gate. We are all of one type.

It is a well laid out amusement, this yard. Toddler water park, splash fountains, water slides, BBQs, cafe and aerobics teachers play gaudy tunes in an indoor hot soup pool.

Something for everybody.

Ham, cheese, and avocado toastie.

Cappuccino. Phone rings, interrupts me, a dinner invitation accepted.

Membership forms complete, token attached to my keyring, dues paid.

I stop writing and get back in the pool, luscious cooling pool.

Day glows orange triangle. A boob popped out.

Ladybug floatie. A cherry red inflated ring with black polka dots holds up the blonde toddler.

Definitely a product of her mother.

Blonde French braids, gel nails, tanned butt.

Adidas shorts in black. Tattoos. Rayban sunglasses. Muscular chest.

Daddies play with their littlest ones.

A mob in the centre. A large group. An indigenous family. Maybe three sets of parents, a dozen children of all ages between the throng. Civil enough, more than civil, happy, attentive to their children, father plays with little ones. Not doing anything different from the other clumps of family fun time.

My neck becomes tense.

I breast-stroke laps in a centre lane. Staying out of the play area with the ramp and step forming the entryway for the non-brace. Those who creep into the chilled pool water. Not like the lap swimmers who dunk straight away into the cordoned-off lane and enjoy the shock. The slope-side is for the playful, the leisurely dog paddler. The social dipper. I crawl six laps and slowly decide on my next stanza. Yes, I will. I will tell you what goes through my mind now during the unhurried relay.

It takes me back to the beginning of last year. 2021.

Maybe I need a coffee for this.

Delay the truth. Hate the words.

Pink plastic jelly watch. Southern stars and skulls inked into the back of a calve.

Two little brothers' ringlets, matching swim shirts, one with a storybook, the other with a teddy bear.

Towels on the grass under a canvas umbrella on a pole. Witches hat covers a drain.

Stop mucking about. Just tell it.

Ok. Back story is unnecessary, I'm a lightweight. A pretty good girl by a regular standard. I don't profess that I'm an angel. There were sins.

But I do have morals, I don't like hurting others in a selfish frenzy/ is that a justification? No, that's getting side-tracked.

In January 2021 I was arrested, I was invited to a private room courtesy of the Queen, for three months. The first time she'd invited me. Before that I had a fairly good run, keeping myself below the radar. I was brought to a Queensland prison stunned. Had not foreseen or expected the attention.

Again, definitely a lightweight. Not enough of a nuisance to be troubled with… but then some traffic infringements could not be ignored. Also, some fines to pay.

I didn't fit in. I didn't know the language. I knew some women there, from my town. Even they were shocked. "How the hell did you get here?". I was always the good girl amongst the blatantly rotten. I didn't take chances or stupid opportunities. My sins were for survival only, essential, deliberate, planned and executed alone.

Once inside the Covid restrictions kept me in isolation for the first week. This was a normal intake procedure for this time. In the second week, observational, we stayed in group unit clusters. Monitored. Checked for behavioural defects. The ability to get along. Follow instructions.

Before the end of week 2, I was deemed socially tolerable by wardens and shifted into Residential 1.

A trial entry into the mainstream population.

Again, I did not know the fucking language. Out of my depth. Unprotected. In a word, prey.

2nd day in Res1. I've always been a loner. Flying under the radar was my skill. Here it was an impediment. Suspicion was aroused. I had always kept myself back from others. Thinking it saved me from conflict. Out of competition with those whose ego's needed the limelight. It had always served me well before. Mouth shut, ears open. Seeing what others were too busy preening to see.

It did not work in this space. People are just like animal's, we can sense fear.

My 'mistake' was walking past a group of indigenous women 'the wrong way'. Socially awkward and trying not to offend I had placed my hand on a miss younger than me, explaining that I was about to open the door to the unit and did not want to bump her with it. She's on the ground close to the door. I was trying to be polite. Unoffensive. They didn't think so.

Whatever the real reason was, three of them followed me to my cell, beat me, kneeing me in my face, and smashing my nose. Blood sprayed across the walls. Another three held guard at my cell door. Ironically, I got on great with them while I helped them to clean up my blood. Shedding clothes and linens to be washed elsewhere. They liked me when they saw that I was cooperative, not a baby.

Alas, intelligence was not great that day. Security cameras in operation gave up the commotion staying silent in my cell post-clean-up was not enough to hide the evidence. Guards soon came to my cell and escorted me to a medical unit where they kept me isolated that night. No medical treatment was administered. The next day I was demoted back to an observation unit, where I stayed until my release three months later.

Crazy twist, the ringleader whose shoulder I touched, she was sent to the same obs. unit and was surprised to see me there. She couldn't understand how this was, as she'd expected my having made a statement to prison guards re the incident, which would have ensured we would have been kept separated for the rest of my stay.

Once realising the lack of statement, she had to acknowledge the power of working CCTV camera's being responsible for the guards finding out and so she promised no one else in the jail would touch me. A reward for my silence. She states to me that she thought I was someone else. Could not remember why she did it. As close to an apology as I would get.

I describe this event, not for spite, but just to illustrate the conflict in terms of my unconscious thinking. Yes, it was a trauma. Yes, I think of it every time I see dark people. No, I don't accept that this reliving of events makes me a racist.

My daughter thinks I am. That's because she is 14 and doesn't understand any explanation I can put into words for her benefit of comprehension.

Technically, I deplore the treatment our country, and our government (in truth ALL the fucked up governing powers across this entire earth) have demonstrated toward coloured humans. It is embarrassing to me that I am descended from animals who were so cruel to others.

Hitler, English, Australian settlers, police, courts, Arab nations, American persecution of Indians, abuse of Chinese, Jews, any minority, African, Aborigines, Ukrainians, and Yemen nationals. Anyone, human or animal that is repressed, hunted, abused, belittled, under classed and bigoted. It all disgusts me. Women's rights. Abuse of powers. Social ignorance. Fucking unacceptable.

Anyone owning a T.V. and switching to SBS world movies or Viceland is unable to deny it. White people messed up. We will spend centuries hopefully 'trying' to make up for the first century here. People raped. Children stolen. At times I cannot comprehend the atrocities that the men that ruled told themselves and the world that it was okay and required, a duty. Bloody wankers. That's the truth of what I think. What we now know.

It does not undo the reality of the world I exist in now.

It does not undo the trauma that I experienced.

It does not justify anything.

It does not deny the memories in my mind that come to light, even when swimming in a relaxed, safe environment with strangers, unaware of me, unknowing my internal thoughts and my mental struggles.

The father plays with his baby and the toddlers. They play in peace. They probably don't even think about me, my presence, oblivious as they luxuriate.

Their opinions are none of my business. I will write my thoughts honestly.

This is my private therapy. Not of importance or interest to anyone else but me.

No need to speak out loud, who would want to? Interpretation by others would depend on their inner fears, demons, experiences, prejudices, ignorance or judgement.

Think what you will. I know what essence is within me. I know my own heart and accept my personal growth as my own. That vented, I will have one last dip in the emptying chlorinated pools and finish up my Sunday afternoon.

Lynd will be here in an hour to pick me up and take me with her to a fellowship meeting at Cooroy. Pizza and people. Blah, blah, blah.

Sunday Evening

Surprisingly not blah, blah, blah. Hmmm...

Lynd was parked outside the pool across the street from the entrance where I stepped out. Towelled off barely, messy unbrushed hair, swollen body, barefoot. Black thigh-length cotton sundress thrown thoughtlessly over swimmers (swimming costume, bathers?).

Perhaps casually as the preference to this shift is because black is slimming, hides flaws and is loose. Nah, it's just easy and better guffaw in my wardrobe of outgrown and ill-styled second-hand bargains.

Lynd, detailed as always. Porcelain skin, neat earrings, jewellery on neck, floral feminine platforms, rinsed and styled mane, and lipstick on, all presented nicely. We drive south on M1 to the Gold Nugget Resturant. A regular dining spot for us. Members of the fellowship come here for dinner on Saturday after our early evening meeting on Stanley Street. It is a routine gathering. This afternoon we only utilise its car park out the front.

The Nugget is attached to a service station so Lynd's little silver hatchback will be safe there until we return. As we wait for our connecting ride, we sit, and Lynd informs me that Lara and Anton will soon arrive and take us to Pomona. She share's the news that Lara's mother passed away the day before however I shouldn't mention it or bring it up in any way. This seems a regular thing amongst my group of acquaintances, who are mostly older than myself. Yes, I think I am one of the youngest that socialises with members outside of the meeting rooms.

The news is sad to hear but has no definitive impact on me. There is no relation, I have not met Lara's mother ever. Also, I have had no comparable maternal relationship in my lifetime. I cannot relate, I don't know what it is to lose someone who would have that mothering role to me. I'm empathetic to grief. I just don't have a mother who would have raised me, loved me or any of the expected virtues that the label mum would imply to any one of the greater populous. It is a simple thing for me to agree to. I don't wish to cause any upset to beautiful Lara. She is an exceptional and caring woman. I admire her partner also. Anton says wise and undisputed reasoning in his testimonies and conversations.

They arrive and we climb into their square bumble-bee-coloured Jeep. A trendy box with its glossy coat.

There appears to be no unusualness in Lara and Anton's demeanour. If I hadn't been informed, I would not have guessed any difference. Conversation flows around the interior, unperceived of any ill emotion. She hides her grief well.

There is talk of directions, the length of the journey, the day's activities of all four present and the destination. We will go to an Italian restaurant that I have not been to before. I haven't been to any other venue or building in Pomona other than the 'Shed' where Sunday night meetings are routinely held. This is intriguing. I haven't been to a good Italian eatery for a few years. A reminder that I usually dine alone and economically.

It is pleasing, the menu delicious, the desserts ordered, and the servings of gourmet pizza wonderful. Nothing to complain about here. Serge is a true Italian, loud, personable, cheery, and confident in his cuisine. The proprietor greets his regulars by name, there is instant familiarity and welcome. Boxes in hand, we strolled to the park benches on the corner of the main street, (all closed storefronts), and we eat from open boxes. Ginger ales, caramel puddings, loaded chicken and olive slices.

Round the bend, into the 'Shed'. Handshakes, hellos, seats taken.

Standards chitchat, people making coffee, the meeting's chairperson dawdles, seated around a table, casual testaments begin. I am comfortable. Well-fed and tired from the earlier swimming and sun. The meeting ends. Chitchat avoided. It can go on and on if you can continue to stand it.

I make the prompts. "I'll be waiting by the car". Lynd and Anton see this, they were waiting for my cue it seems, glances, goodbyes, out to the darkened carpark trot, trot, trot. Where is Lara? Always the chit-chatter, God love her we will grace her with patience tonight. Here she is. All aboard. I'm not a talker but happy to be, easily at the moment. Lara makes it easy. They are good people.

Deposited at the service station, cars swapped. Lynd drives me to my flat. I am fulfilled, a full day. Graced. A Sylvester Stallone drama is on the television as I climb into bed. All the running in my mind has slowed to a calm, a peace. Close my doors, my blinds. Fans on a timer, I lay. I am calm. Mind not on ski's.

Despite this sleep evades me. I rise at midnight, cigarette.
Relaxation music on lowest volumes. I am overcome.

Monday

Routine, business, alarm, shower, appointment,

Stationary supply store, home, pack bag. Plot across tracks and
fields, gymnasium, and swimming pool.

Chit chat, chai latte, adaptive, Becker on low hubbub, a nap.
Fans on.

4 pm, shower, Laurence. Black SUV, fellowship, lost keys, fans
on.

Home again little pig. Fans on.

Cigarette. SBS world movies.

Lulled to sweaty sleep. Fans on. Toss and turn. This is not real
sleep; I can still hear the windmills turnings. Pick up the remote,
cup of herbal tea, cigarette, remote, and fans off the timer. I let
it run. The best lines of the day come to me. I'm too desperate
to let sleep follow the calm state and breathing, so I file them
away.

Tuesday Morning

How amazing, dedicated to the project, entertaining my theory that this purging of words is going to be key in relieving my mind's endless looping over some thoughts. Give me the prescribed reliefs. It does distract. Call to form. Negligent.

Toilet, kettle, cigarette, and impermanent sentences form across topics but not yet forming the subjects or circumstances I had hoped to illustrate in chapters.

Explain, make a record of, order, and exonerate. An explanation to myself of my inner hell. The torture replayed, slow shaping of my character. Let us just jump on and get the awfulness out of my fingers. The concepts of determined explanations. Who do I need to explain this to? No one I know.

Creativity aside, I'll just put it down. Rip the band aid off.

The news of Lara's mother passing has no devastating effect on me. It merely provides an opening to the subject. An opportunity.

The lack of any mother.

That's a new description. See, ordered my thought stream already. Quickly now no more dilly-dallying. This is the shit part.

Kay was 14 or 15. She lived with her younger sister, Chelle. A hard-working practised mother, Vale. A carefree slacker Joseph. That's the details told to me. Vale was one of the first women inducted to an education for female nurses, I'm told it was an initiative of the present government in the early 1970s, again. This is just the legend passed down to me in recounts of events.

Not researched facts. Children believe to be gospel the things they are told, accept them as a given. Joseph smoked pot, dicked about. Worked intermittently. Fathered two girls to his headstrong wife.

Vale carried the reins, stronger in will. Determined to make successful her decisions. In a changing decade, carried the family and developed a career to support the household unit created. Late nights, long shifts. A certain tiredness came along with determination and ambitions. Perhaps no ambitions as much as survival. The dole and pensions were not yet in existence. Government income assistance was just becoming developed, mostly in the form of an after-war supplement. The veterans laid the foundation of need after World War II. Simply put, Vale held it all together. Held them up. Her strength overtakes her motherly role.

There's a recount about Joseph, one time he lost his job and didn't want to admit such to Vale, the successor so he got dressed every day and went to sit on a park bench, feeding pigeons until his folly was discovered. There was no elaboration when I was told this, it characterised him adequately and anyway, I was a child who asked very few questions. Conversations and explanations were not bestowed on me often. Similar to Kay in that regard, the absence of adult-child communications. Though for very different reasons.

Kay had the family unit. But not the parent with the capacity for coddling. The situation did not allow for it. Vale was so busy ticking all the boxes, she was absent while Kay experimented with boys, seeking comfort and attention in other places. Once in a drug-fuelled haze, Kay did tell me about my father, that she had brought her beau to the family home. Had sex with him in the kitchen, Joseph was in residence, in the lounge room or garage. Vaguely doing his own things most likely not even aware that his two daughters were home.

Such was his input. This was in Orange.

Months later, Vale moved the family North to the top of the border of the state to Murwillumbah, NSW. In some advancement to her career, I think as Head of the Radiology or x-ray department. I do not know which hospital. Sometime there, on the border of Queensland, the Sunshine State where temperatures were high and sun-soaked, Vale bluntly asked Kay if she was fat or just had a cold. This not-so-gentle enquiry was due to the oversize bulky jumpers Kay was donning. An ignorant or naive attempt to hide a swelling abdomen. This was me.

The recent geography became a bonus, Vale, using the opportune move to be allowed to create some plausible story. Something along the lines of making Kay wear Vale's wedding ring and covering the absence of the husband with a story of my father going to war and not returning. A believable scenario for the day and times.

Many men didn't return from the war. It was just tragic enough to deter any insensitive further questions from lookie-loo's. It was a period when morals and standards of social conduct were still important to social standings, reputations could be scraped off the floor with a little white lie and a feigned dignity. Vale was fierce, no one was going to puncture this farce not to her face anyway. She would have torn them down. The next is pretty simple.

A later geographical back to Orange, NSW. Where the same cover story could be used in reverse when the foursome, now five, arrived back in the south, Kay was moved to a Caravan Park with this baby, a child herself with no idea what she was doing.

Wait, I must put in here another story I heard. Before I go too far ahead. Josephs' later second wife and Aunt Chelle did tell me something when I was 10 years old, some amusing note about how Vale and Joseph had gone calling on my father's parents and were not received well. My paternal grandparents informed my maternal grandparents that they were perhaps the fourth set of minders, who has felt the humiliating necessity to make such a visit and introduction. They weren't having a bar of it. planned to send their son overseas imminently to avoid war, or avoid too early parenthood, I do not know.

So that's it, my illustrious family history. The stretched-out course of it is something scatty to be excepted. Kay messed up. Was going to continue messing up.

Another piece of the pie. This one was relayed by the stepfather, Michel.

1976, grotty working-class hotel, some chaptered bike club members, piss and vinegar, whiskers and unwashed jeans, some underage girls drinking. Some local constables come through the bar, routine checks, a country town. A wolf whistle, young men whisking the underage drinkers onto the backs of their motorcycles to evade the law.

They are drunk, it's all-youthful fun. Piss and bluster.

Michel rides Kay to her place, in the caravan park.

There is a baby, alone in the van crying, who had likely been alone for hours. Michel astounded, bound by moral duty, bundles them up and takes them home with him to his father's orchard property in a small town south of Orange, instant family, I then lived in Borenore, NSW.

Kay and Michel married two years later. I wouldn't discover that he was not my father for another eight years. No one could count in the early 1980's apparently and by then Kay had delivered me a brother and sister.

I was not permitted at the wedding for photos were evidence opposing the essential fable. There was once in existence a solitary photograph of me in a dress, hidden behind the bridal cars on a gravel driveway, with the chapel in the background. Vale took this photograph. Any person who may have found it would not find any evidence to prove it was taken the same day. There are no adults in the background of the picture, or beside me to betray the social faux pas. The ceremony and reception photos didn't reveal anything of me. An unmentioned secret.

Shortly after the birth of Emily in 1983, Kay left her children, the farm, and her marriage. I only have one memory I can date to this period. It was observing a domestic argument between Kay and Michel. Kay shouting arguments. Michel takes his frustrations out on a wood pile and chopping block under the diesel tank stand at the bottom of the driveway, sheds on either side of them. A gate onto a horse paddock was in my view behind them. I believe the marriage was afflicted with these upsets. Michel's father has died, leaving him the barren useless orchard, him working the farm, her youth and dissatisfaction adding to the hard rural existence.

Presently, now is not the moment to dwell in history. The morning begins in a rush. I slept late, dawdled over breakfast of herbal tea. Heat oppressing, promising to get higher, a blister. Thankfully I will be quartered in air conditioning for most of the day. Beep Beep. My ride is outside, I'm not dressed. Highly unusual, not an occurrence of mine since I moved here.

Oops, sundress overhead, toothbrush in the handbag. Floral shirt, sandals, fan off, door locked. Downstairs, away, an older member drives at 20km an hour and I feel like I'm hostage to a detailed account of their week. This is what I think... oh.

Fellowship meetings, a study of our spiritual progress.

Council meeting, I'm the present treasurer. Accounts given, reimbursements, minutes recorded, all in agreement. The heat causes us to dispense with drawn-out formalities. Business in order. Christmas week planned out, dates mentioned and confirmed.

Now the pleasure part, book shopping, painting and art supplies, chemist, groceries. Goldfield's shopping centre. I take advantage of completing these errands whilst I am being driven home, en route. Fresh produce refrigerated, books on the shelf, materials stored in cupboards, accounts and ledgers restored to closet space.

A ham and cheese Danish, I load my medications, dose, and injected. Stay dressed, walking down the hill, banking done, library, emails, calls made, home again, home again, little pig.

It's 4 o'clock, and the temperature and humidity is excessive. Dress off, cold shower, curtains drawn. Coolness keeps me indoors now. It's been a busy day, too late for the gymnasium, pool or any other destinations. Intent to closest myself inside till daylight comes tomorrow. I press on the television, breathe out and lay in a daze for an hour or so before that thoughts creep in. I leisurely put ideas into order.

Now nightfall, I make noodles for one and pick up my pen. Hurried descriptions, today's activities were briefly mapped down. I'm at ease, not forced to be rested, to rest or be mobile. I take a few hours just existing. Waves of heat attempt to crawl under the curtain's hem into the room, blocked by immobile shade, I do not ruffle anything. Disgruntled, strained.

Voices pass by my windows, and doors in the carpark slam shut. I ignore everything and everyone outside of my unit. I don't envy anyone outside in the street tonight.

The air slowly cools. Thunder rumbles in the distance. I take it easy. My body regulates itself to my new medicine. I hydrate. None of the predicted side effects occur in me it is a blessing. I am thankful. I am grateful for my surroundings; quiet and comfortable I enjoy this evening viewing knowing I have done all my next 'right things'. Serenity.

I watch Everybody Is Fine starring Robert De Niro. A man retired, his four adult children living their lives in New York City, too busy with careers, lives, families and loves. His determination to connect with them is something I can relate to. Everybody Is Fine. If he can't get them to come to him, then he will for to them.

Next door's bass vibrates through our adjoining brick walls. I can't hear the actual music, just feel the physical thump alerting me to the presence of music.

I'm used to it like a heavy mental massage.

Sweat trickles down my spine slowly, I brush my back with my hand before I absorb what it actually is.

Dove grey painted vintage bed. Charcoal sheets, stone-coloured comforter. Silver satin and sequined cushions, fluffy footstool, chrome and black ceramic lamp base, antique store sourced hard covers in stacks above fragrance bottles and my pearl earrings swing from a lone martini glass on my dresser. A round mirror hangs from a black ribbon, on vintage ceramic door handles refurbishing the armour.

Metal trimmed wooden travel chest, French style font, stencilled flowers, a white rail with silver hooks supporting a dozen brown, tan, and beige totes, purses, and shoulder bags. All different, all the same hues. Folded soft dove-coloured throws, stacked on the too-small chair. Closed doors, an island within my cocoon. My painted abstract nude forms hang on walls on three sides of my vault. Navy window curtains block any views, in or out.

Floral shirt slung over doorknob, gold thongs on the floor beside the bed. The same dove-shaded floor beneath it all. I created this space. Everything is in its place. Not over cluttered, no space is wasted, I own everything I use, could desire to use. Nothing is out of place. My possessions total the exact measurement of what I use, and what I need. There is nothing, nothing that I would want for in this collection of my things that are all precisely mine and all of me.

A constructed environment allows perfect use, the tolls of my creativity.

I am a whole personality here. This room is a map of myself and my activities. I hover inside my cube. It holds me, safe and secure. It nurtures me and allows me to build my installations, write my bowers, depict my visions. Houses my growth and shapes my sanity. Disguises my uncertainty, gives pause to my regrets and welcome's a veil over a proposed reality.

The rain falls now. This movie has turned sad. Everything seems fitting today, each moment, each segment and all same its interfolding parts are placed acutely.

De Biro has a heart attack. I open the curtains. Give my fan's motor a break. I listen to the water hitting the street, the tarred road out front. The rain breaks in the movie too.

So, apt. on-time, co-ordinated. Surreal. Everything's fine. Lighting cracks. Water slows its fall. Steady now, the volume is muted, the sound turned down. The evening is perfectly mirrored in the movie.

My mattress is firm on one side, sagged, or pushed own on the other side. The rain pitter-patters now.

A cigarette, screen door locked. I turn the television off with my remote. The children find their own way. I pray. I sleep.

Not real sleep but a cinematic slide of unremembered dreams, never captured as a whole a complete story upon waking. Within minutes dilute into themes, flashes, not able to keep complete enough to transcribe onto paper.

I toilet, lay down again. Decide if I'm really here. Still here. Stuck with this I slide into…

Wednesday Morning

Motionless. Paused. The never-ending monotony of consciousness. Minutes pass. Motionless. Undecided.

Thoughts begin to creep in. Begin to form. I fight to pull off waking, the stream of endless days. I reach for my mobile phone. Turn data on. Confirm opening hours for my pool. Dreams slipped off, can't recall the story. I know I didn't like it, as usual, a barrage of people and scenes of a former lifetime. 6 AM. The pool opened half an hour ago. This suits me. Gives me my destination. Up. Up, I go.

Tracksuit on, fruit retrieved from the crisper drawer. Water, injection, and books in the bag. Creams, sunblock, and hair not brushed still atop my head in a knot from the day before. From days before.

The dealer neighbour has a caller. Swear words, demands. The females that come there are always noisy and announce to all residents their arrivals, business, then departure.

Phone into the bag. The balcony door is locked. Stepping out onto landing at front. I see two sets of feet through banisters, on the 2nd stairwell.

The 6ft scruff of my neighbour's face, is most often congenial. I have had no problems with the men themselves. I smile. He smiles.

"It's Norris, isn't it?'

"Yes". He steps forward.

"Do you think your female visitors could be a little... (I pause for effect) ... less boisterous?" We chuckle.

It is not a full reprimand just banter.

"Just tell them to shut the fuck up". He laughs.

Jovial, he enjoys that I have spoken to him. I am always silent, and not social with this group.

"I can't do that; they are your friends! I just don't get why the girls have to announce themselves from the street. 'Hi, I'm here, I'm on show'".

They all laugh now. Not at me, but because they think these same thoughts also. All is well, a moment of camaraderie. I descend the stairwell and plod off down the path. Better to have these fixtures, than to put them offside into hostile status. Smirking they call goodbye.

Round the corner, up the slanted cross, the T-section, "Good morning", "Good morning". The local business owners on the top of the hill arrive for a day's propriety on Mellor St.

Suma Suma Café.

Trendy, bustles, vintage barn doors rough, unrepaired, propped on trestles, line the pavement creating a table large enough to put 20 to 30 bottoms. I see diners breakfasting at one end. I walk to the other, and seat myself solitary. Place my bag and enter to order my cappuccino.

I stopped buying coffee and sweetened Matcha, tea and syrups months ago. I also forgo sugar.

I was consuming a kilogram a fortnight, switching to herbal teas. The premise being to cut down on calorie consumption. Despite the effort, I managed to gain another three kilograms onto my gut.

Stay in the day, stay in the day. Will I bore you with descriptions of the weather and environment? Yes, I will. I'll regress or continue. However, you may feel about it.

The rain of last night has cut the heat, the shine from the sky above so cutting that clouded grey-white hurts my eyes so that dark glasses are my necessity, not my accessory.

This café warrants some explanation. I enjoy this space. Perched one side of the bridge, the bridge carries the tarmac of Mellor Street up over the tracks, giving an eye-level side view into the platform of the Mary Valley Rattler, a tourist destination, historical railway buildings, no further in use a travel destination. This is not a part of the transport system of Queensland anymore. Now a tourist trap. Over-budget wine and cheese platters on locomotives, restored, revived, relived. Below the platform's edge, ground level of the bridge sits the Gympie Family History Society Inc. slightly above average amateur murals of gold diggers, pioneers in bonnets, convicts and mock wanted posters that decorate brick wall alongside the Society doors leading the countrified picturesque in to the under platform train tunnel, the pedestrian walkway to Tozer St, alternatively halfway up an alcove, stone stairs lead up to the old platform, to where I sat on Sunday morning on route to the pools.

Let me not get too far away from where I am at present.

I attempt to stay in the day.

Gingers Fruit Farm van pulls up and has left the motor running, doors open, on the curb of the gutter in front of me. Deliveries were carried inside by a blonde lady (clearly a fruit fan. Not an ounce of fat evident on her frame, gym shorts of Lycra and cut sleeves t-shirt).

Traffic increases around and past us, past me. People begin their day, choofing off to work, attentions, the hum in the air of motors comes to me, unaware of the peace from half an hour ago.

I check my phone, it's 8 AM.

Elderly hippy cruises into the gutter, peddles stopping. Helmet on, coasts to the driveway and finds a fence. Fastens his bike.

A middle-aged couple with token pair of Chihuahua's, candy pink collars and musk stick lolly dog leads, pink purse attached to one's dog lead. The second Chihuahua sits on the male owner's lap, and sports a tiny pair of angel wings, again in shiny pink, the same shade. Novel. A waitress pats them. She thinks it is cute. I think contrived. I'm not an animal person.

I don't seek to replace empty nests with fur babies and substitutes.

No children mean no children. You've got to feel that shit. Or you'll never get through it.

They are at the next, adjoining trestle table, further, along at the other end a mum in her late twenties caringly explains educational information to her couple of little girls.

The history of photography she teaches them, "When I was a little girl, we didn't take so many photographs, a camera was used. The pictures cost money and were not on a screen, able to be edited, deleted…".

Her vein explanation that images were printed, kept in a book, cherished, uncomprehended ideas float over the top of toddlers' heads, not settling into brains. I lift my head, I smile, and the couple next to me share a glance and acknowledge my amusement.

I liken this to explaining air flight or space travel to a resident of the 1840s. inconceivable. Unimagined. Mum doesn't give up, uncaring if the information is not conceived. She has delivered it and done the education to some satisfaction. Comforted by the belief that somewhere, someday in the future these little snippets of information will link up and create some knowledge of facts.

Family departs, couple with fur-family clink cups and retreat to cars.

Waitress's clear.

The owner takes a moment to sit with regular customers. Men in non-stop conversations, absorbed in the company of the other. Laughter. Talks of an event at work yesterday.

Espresso Bar and Design Collective.

Speckles of water float across my page. Women in tailored skirts and business blouses. Classic earrings, precious metals, neat wristwatch. Compact black leather purse. Navy blue and black. Leather flats. Contrasted by teenage wait staff, matching lycra shorts, pictures of Queensland health. Bodies that are healthily tanned by the sun in the sunny state.

We are inland to the beaches, in a rural setting, but still a part of the Sunshine Coast.

This café gives the feel to me of Newtown venues, art cafés, Gold Coast, and modern casual living.

Ribcage high, matt black, ceramic, oversized plant pots adorn gutter-side pillars (supporting overhead veranda), rudely housing brown dried weeds, native seeds of wild grass, overflowing and bereft of flowers. It seems an obscene oversight, but somehow deliberate. The attention directed to customer service, outer details unhindered, and rough, remind us of our rural existence.

Country homes on either side of the Soma Soma entrance, their front fence built 200 years ago of huge sandstone blocks typical of this place. Home residents and businesses interspersed with history, crude, essential architecture, and weatherboard-building rock-solid entrances. Multiple coats of paint over the handrail, rail bridge, and weathered beams. Aloe vera, yucca's under Poinciana, Elm, power pole, cable lines.

All this is floating around me, at the same time absorbed into me, I'm soaking it in.

There are many details inside, style, decoration, and curios, I postpone them for another time, my sense is adequately full enough from the outside moments.

Beach towel over the shoulder, I hold the date, coffee finished, I walk on. Footbridge to my right. Good morning, Gympie.

Beach towel over the shoulder, calico shoulder bag. Tunnel. Platform. Brief stop at the Gympie Men's Shed, a not-for-profit community group providing usefulness to retirees. Repurposed, repaired, restored, and recreated home furniture and garden ware on sale in the chain link yard attached. I joke with the 90-year-old overzealous busybodies. Are they unaccustomed to females inside these walls? I guess so.

I prefer to use a credit card. I mark my items for delivery. Two trestles and a garden gate door for myself, similar to the Soma Soma furniture I just sat at, same colour trestles, the same colour, same paint job door/tabletop similar condition. These are ideal to set up in my loungeroom come workspace. This will be in place of getting a dining table. Portable and large enough to support a large double-stretched canvas.

On to the gym/pools, via Andrew Fisher Park (incidentally this is also my cousin's name).

Gumtree, Gumtree, Hibiscus.

Peony, Staghorn, Pansy.

Past Nevil's empty driveway. Steel and glass automatic gates. Refill a glass water bottle. Café chairs. Notes.

Gymnasium. Mearle grey hooded swears, Asic's on.

Bubble-gum disinfectant. Benny and the Jetts. Sky hooks. (Is this appropriate music for a workout? Oh, yeah right, we are in Gympie. My bad).

The Cure, Rhythm Cats. Midnight something or other. Lola.

Lulling me to sleep instead of into action.

Sanitising spray. Chux super wipes.

Christmas baubles sticky taped to blackboard and interior doors.

A poster proclaims 'Every journey has its beginning. BEGIN'. An apt paragraph.

We are here to support you and set you on the path to success to achieve your goals. Our qualified and experienced... blah blah…. Stay motivated… blah blah… journey with us.

Shoulder press. Leg extension.

Kriz and Nevil were curious why I've stopped and gone to notepad inside the gym. Too polite to ask.

They smirk, assuming I'm buying time.

I am.

Solomon glides through the door another member of our fellowship. He hellos and farewells on either side of his swim time.

Smiling.

Encouragement.

The physical therapy instructor comes over to upgrade my session time.

I assure her that I'm not leaving. Expect that I will pause often.

15 minutes here, 15 minutes there.

Nevil knows me, almost well enough now not to bother disturbing me.

My business is my own.

I do not allow directing, questioning or coaching.

Solomon does not. He enquires. I throw off. Solomon departs.

Jan and Peter arrive, fully clothed. Chit chat. I leave them to it at the Kiosk table and chairs.

Sunscreen, nectarine, chlorine.

Kriz and Nevil leave Peter, and Jan departs for shopping errands.

Patches of sky blue dispense the greys. Whitened puffs, piped in, meringue shaped.

Sky-high towers of spotlights.

No birds are present, hidden above the awning.

Hot pink eye goggle strap.

Piggyback.

"Get off".

Marron bandeau-bikini top.

Ponytails. Browned lizard skin.

Golden lone earring on the blue tile below the water in the pool. 50 meters. Duck dive. Board shorts. Peaked cap. Water bottle Fitbit watch. Timer ticks. Breaststroke. Crawl, crawl, crawl.

Skull cap. Handicap.

Unhand my sister. Best behaviour.

No running. Smack, smack, smack.

Chlorine green, a natural blonde.

Steel brace. Blue, purple rinse.

Adjustable strap. Checked messages.

Foam noodle. Bath towel. Tradies work shirt, blue and yellow strip. Lap, lap, lap.

French braid. Pidgeon appears on an electrical cable. Flip-flop. Scrunchie. Saving water. Saving energy. Sunbather pool cover systems. No diving. Medium lane.

Caution shallow water. Conditions of use.

I forget myself. I complain. I am Rhoda from Virginia's 'The Waves'. I am Susan, my friends depart.

I stay. Business not done. Skin is not baked.

Perspiration drips as I forego the water, the umbrella, and the café awning. I cook in the sun. A deliberate purge of salted ducts.

Marco polo. I answer no one. My choice to solitude in my defiance. My prerogative. There are words to assemble, clearing of thoughts in cooled watery lanes, alternating with gifted prose that needs to be downloaded. Sunk into my head and hopes to be remembered. I rinse in niceness, fry in turn, injecting words of prized literature, discarding, and shedding throughs of my own making.

Willing the product to emerge from the balled top of my Papermate biro, help me produce, teach me. Make me worthwhile. I pray not for humankind and world peace. I pray to be worthwhile to have some wonderful things to contribute to the masses on this spinning ball. I pretend that this is a real possibility. When in all likely hood I will abandon this project minutes before completion. Saving me from the prospect of failure. To postpone is excusable, failure, and lack of talent, are inexcusable, I will avoid confirmation of my lack of talent. Hide under the sheets from it. Find to breath underwater.

Half the day is wasted in reprisals and barbs.

Chip dish, gravy in a plastic pot. Ants circulate. A cigarette outside the gates. Melancholy grabs me. I gather my shirt sides over my bathers. Re-enter. Rinse and repeat.

Little boys wrestle, dunk, dunk it off.

Gravity grasps my entire body and drags me down like a substantial physical weight. Jesus Christ, please save me. Another hour and I may be lost.

Grief circles in the background. I am cast. My neck and throat tighten. Please, God, wash it off.

As soon as my ankles, and calves slide into the regenerative coolness of the water, the pool begins its baptism. I am washed. The white ring, red bands of North, South, East and West gripping the lifebuoy hanging from a pole, poolside, in case of emergency. The analogy is not lost on me. Forty minutes of methodical lapping brings me around. Saves my immortal soul.

Refreshed, revived. A more positive feeling in the chest. Caws, squawks. Young natural re-head girl in token pink. A sun-stripped brunette playmate in leopard, cheetah print. Some things are a given. R.S.L. ladies finish afternoon water aerobics. A physical physiologist and lifeguard push a trolley of equipment back to its position in a storage room.

I muse, and wonder, what direction I am taking in these passages.

Whether is it a book, a novel, or a diary, definitely is not a destination or travel guide. I wish I had the formal education in literature, any vague indication of how to label or characterise this rambling that forms 'something' out of an empty notepad. How many words are needed, with mirth I deny any knowledge of a possible ending. Does it speak for itself? Am I giving written evidence of a mad woman? I smile. All I am sure of is the working out of myself as a '20th-century woman' in recovery, an activity living out her definition of The Twelfth Step. Somewhere along the way, I gathered about me some principles. Now I incorporate them into daily living. Honestly, though the product of this would have a more tangible feel. A solid feel. A halt to the slide and effect of not having awareness of principles.

I can dream, trick myself into believing, and anticipate answer's that I imagined somewhat between. There I go complaining again. I've really got to work on that. I do. I will. I have. 'Progress not perfection'. A concept that promises a cure. A cure from the 'Malady of the Mind'. (that's more fucking like it).

My mind is a steering-wheel, my actions are the overriding G.P.S. I'm not doing too bad. I hear myself laughing with friends and have to admit that I'm still alive. Ability to function, survive, conquer the other moments of unrest, insecurity, impatience, routine self-imposed detest.

www.ingramcontent.com/pod-product-compliance
Lightning Source LLC
Chambersburg PA
CBHW070625120726
47909CB00004B/1330